Western Novels by G. R. Howe

No Time To Trust

Dragons Of Fire

Crow Woman On Deadman

Tequila Promises

No Chance

Rumors

Books and photos available at:
www.emptysaddles.com

Short Stories
Out of Kane

G. R. Howe

Revised Edition 2018

iv

Acknowledgements

I thank those who took their valuable time to read and edit the manuscript. Their comments and suggestions were invaluable. Thanks especially to my chief critic and grammarian, Joy Howe, who has lived with every word. Special thanks as well to Martha Howe, Heidi Hart, and Rachel Montgomery.

For Joy

A WORK OF FICTION

These individual short stories are not intended to be an accurate historical account of actual events. They are definitely works of fiction created on a string of successive mornings from a single word, a convoluted thought and a desire to string them both together in a semblance of coherency. Except for those elements which are true, they are mostly figments of my imagination

Several of these short stories are based on the lives of actual people who spent some time living in the shadows of the Big Horn Mountains. Also stories I heard my Dad, my Uncle Joe, Uncle Virgil, and my great uncles tell. Even the truth as I see it, feel it, smell it, and hear it, is a figment of something. I have no idea what. I leave it to you, the reader, to sort it out. Somewhere in the shadows of a leafless cottonwood you might find something worth keeping, a tale worth telling, perhaps worth remembering.

There is my disclaimer.

As in everything, there are exceptions and that exception in this collection is the short story entitled "Bill And Me." That one, and frankly, several others are true. If, for some reason you wish to doubt the "Bill And Me" story--trying as we did to grow up in what was left of Kane, Wyoming--ask

Bill. Since forever he has been a better storyteller than I. He may have seen those events differently than I. Maybe not. I can tell you this: his story will definitely be better than mine. Believe this much: without him there would have been no story. I toned down the events I described. In some cases, way down. So ask him. Although he left Kane, Wyoming as we all were forced to do, he's still there.

TABLE OF CONTENTS

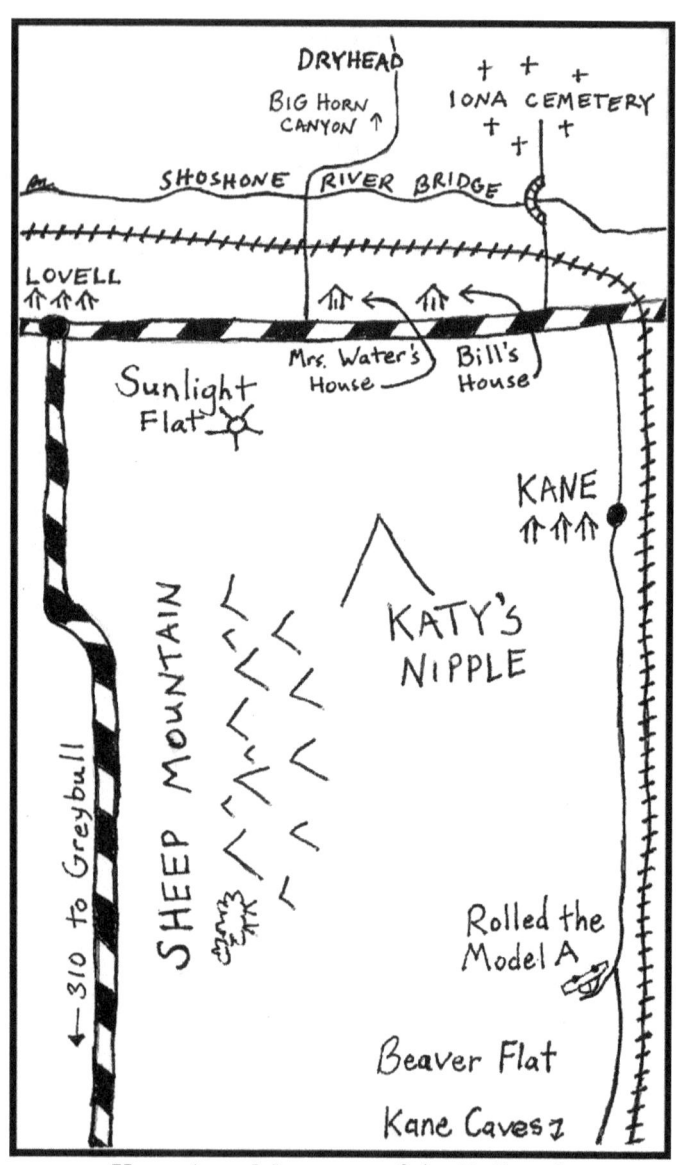

Kane Area Map west of the Railroad

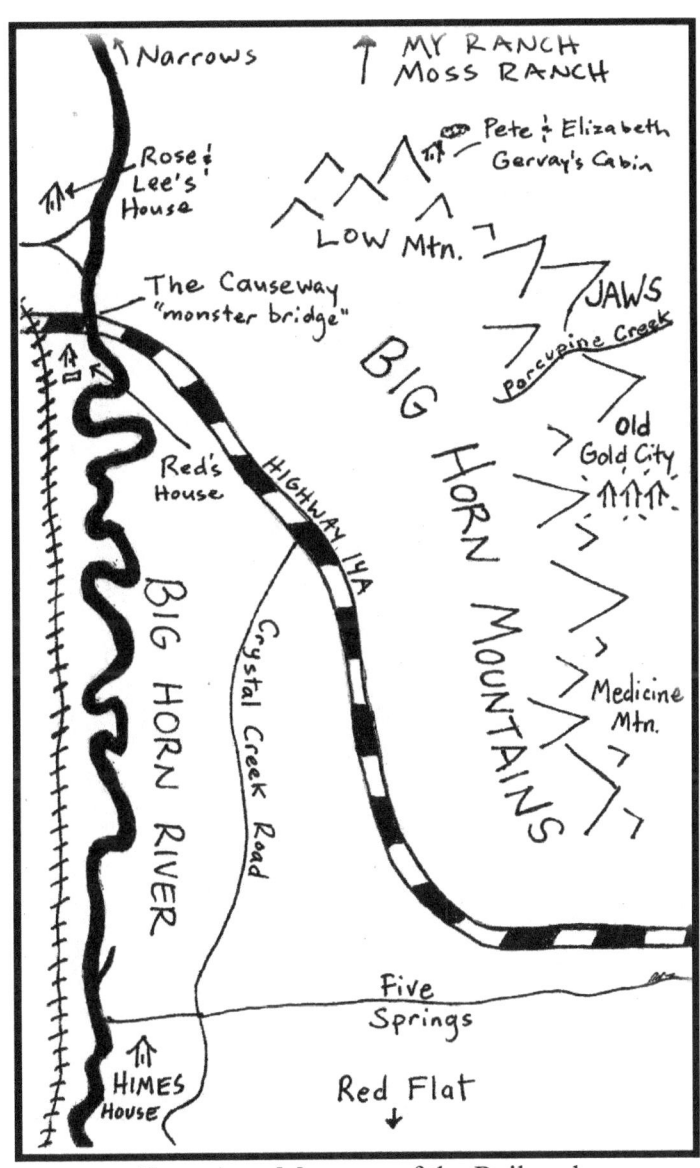

Kane Area Map east of the Railroad

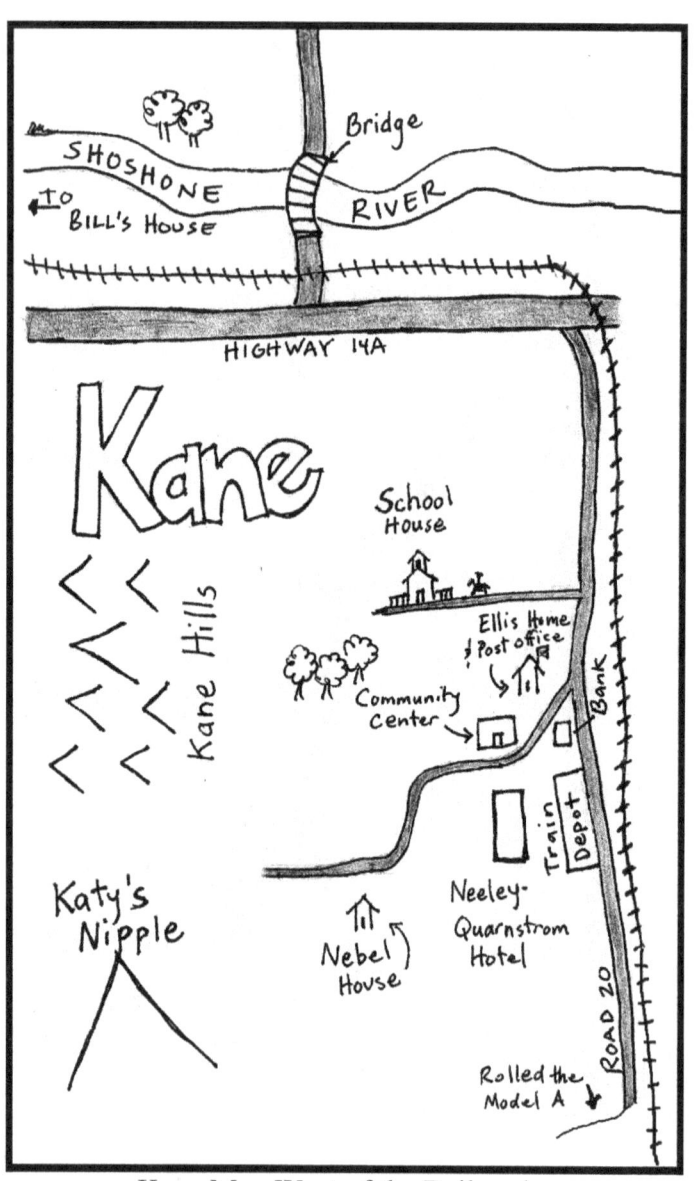

Kane Map West of the Railroad

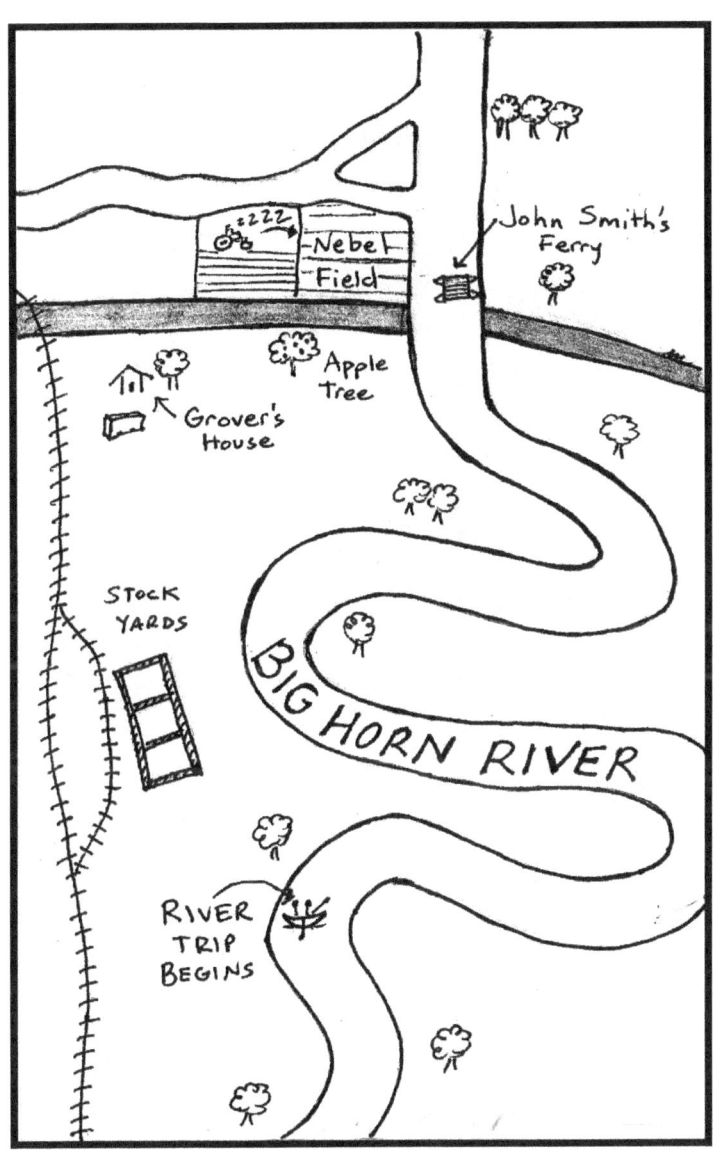

Big Horn River east of Kane

Preface

If a short story is a picture window of life when it's not a pretty picture, then these stories are the not-so-pretty stories of life in Kane, Wyoming. Kane, unlike most other towns, had a beginning and an ending. It sprang into existence some time in the 1880s and died ignominiously in 1965. That made it unique. Thus, these stories are the convoluted thoughts and visions of what once was and never will be again. The poet, Marta, in describing children said: "Some are happy, Some are sad, All designed to drive you mad." This collection has that in mind.

CHAPTER 1

OLD MAN AT THE FERRY

Preface

In the spring the bands came to the Kane Flat, not the kind with flutes and banjoes but those with hundreds of sheep followed by bearded men, some leading their horses; some not. Each herd was followed at a distance by light green, wheeled, canvas covered wagons drawn by teams of horses. The wagons carried beds and small cooking stoves, with hidden drawers for pots and pans, and bags of flour, sugar, coffee beans and cans of corn and peaches. The sheep wintered on the flats west of Cowley and Byron and farther up river until the need for grass became unsurmountable and they had to move.

In early April the bands came to the Kane ferry, one after another seeking passage cross the Big Horn River to the green pastures beyond. They'd arrive amid boiling dust, darting dogs and cursing sheepherders. Sometimes the herds arrived so quickly they'd stack up until by afternoon there'd be ten or fifteen bands spread out on the west side of the river, waiting their turn at the ferry. One after another, the herdsmen were greeted by the ferryman, and sometimes by his boys when they weren't in

1

school or simply didn't go--staying at home to work the river with the old man

The ferryman went by the name of John Smith. Every year he'd make a little money ferrying sheep across the Big Horn River. Five dollars would buy him several sacks of coffee beans and a new shirt, not to mention flour, salt, 44-40 cartridges and a small sack of hard rock candy. The rest of the year he'd take folks across or bring them back when asked. While he was idle he'd plug up holes in the ferry to keep her from sinking. Before winter set in he'd pull it out of the river. The river ice would crush her sides if he didn't.

Big Horn River Ferry at Kane

3

My favorite short story author is Ernest Hemingway. He set the standard. If he had visited Kane in 1908, this is the story that he would have written.

"Imitation is the sincerest of flattery."
-Charles Caleb Colton, 1820

My business was across the Big Horn River. The Cattlemen's Association hired me to make sure the sheep herds stayed north of the Cottonwood Canyon drift fence and on Little Mountain pastures. They figured cows didn't like salt sage anyway and sheep weren't worth a shooting war, provided they stayed north of the drift fence.

To get across I put my horse in the river south of the Smith ferry. He walked the shallows until it got deep. When he started swimming I pushed myself off the horse's hind end and grabbed hold of his tail. It's best not to get yourself kicked to death if you can help it. I did that so's not to have to wait for space on the ferry and to save a dime. It cost two-bits for me, my horse and the damn dog to make use of Smith's ferry. Two bits was two bits and I never was too sure about the dog getting himself on board. He was a bit notional. A number of times he refused to get on the ferry even though his passage was paid for and the space was no extra bother. I figure he didn't like the way the ferry felt underfoot. Like I said, he was notional.

Once on the east side I waited for the dog and for me and my horse to dry out. It was comfortable standing in the sunlight watching the ferryman loading sheep on the other side of the river. As soon as he got a couple of head on board the rest invariably followed. Until then it was sure a fight. In the warmth of the morning sun, steam would lift from the horse's neck, shoulders, and flanks.

After I had waited a few minutes, I got anxious to finish my business so I started walking, leading the horse. The dog could catch up if he was of a mind. A hundred yards from the river I came across a dusty old man sitting under the stark branches of a cottonwood. There was no shade to speak of for the tree had barely started to green up. He was wearing a shabby sheepskin torn at the pockets and pulled tight around his shoulders. His head was covered by a felt hat stretched and worn down around the edges. A faded yellow slicker covered his legs and the tops of a pair of worn down at the heel boots that had seen better days a long time ago. He was dusty from the passing bands of sheep. He didn't look like he had moved for some time.

I saw him and nodded as I approached. He didn't move.

"You all right?" I asked because he sure didn't look all right.

He looked up, his grey eyes taking the full measure of me without responding.

"You eaten?" I asked.

He shook his head no.

I found some jerky in my saddlebags and handed it to him but he didn't take it. I left it sitting on the log beside him and commented on the weather and how I'd never seen so many sheep. When I looked back he'd picked up the jerky.

"I didn't feed the cat," he said rubbing the jerky between his fingers.

"What?" I said.

"I didn't feed the pigeons. There was no more wheat. No barley. Nothing at all. Didn't feed the cat. I didn't."

There was no sense to his talk so I mounted, pulling myself around so I could see the feller. He didn't say anything more.

"Have a good one," I said. I touched the reins to the bay's neck. He came around smartly and I let the bay have his head. The dog was out in front. I wondered how that dog got there without me seeing him.

Took me all day to finish my business. I came back to the river early evening, having ridden the drift fence east to west, to the mouth of the canyon and back. Nothing was out of order. The old man was still sitting on the downed log in the stand of cottonwood trees. Smith had shut his ferry business down for the moment. I could see him sitting in his makeshift shack, a coffee cup in hand. The smell of it drifted in the breeze. It had me longing for a cup. Across the river another band of sheep had worked its way up to the loading dock. The dogs were holding them, keeping them standing or milling in circles, waiting on the ferry and the ferryman's cup of coffee.

"How you doing, Old Timer?" I asked, stepping down from the bay. The dog stood off to the side growling.

The old man nodded.

I handed him another piece of jerky and what I had left of a sourdough biscuit. He took the jerky, rubbing the surface with calloused fingers as if he were brushing dust off it. The half-eaten biscuit he set on the log beside him.

"Looks like this is it for me," he murmured.

I stared at him a moment, then asked if he wanted a drink of water. He didn't reply.

"Where you from?"

"Old Gold City," he said, seemingly taking pride in that fact. "I stayed until the gold petered out, til the last man left. Nobody's there now. Everyone's gone. Snow's deep.

"What did you do up there?" I asked. Old Gold City was at ten thousand feet, maybe a little more depending where you chose to stand. It was still winter at that elevation. It never warmed up until the first of June.

"Livery stable," he said slowly. "No one's there. No horses to shoe. Liveryman just walked away. Left me with the cat and the pigeons. Gold petered out," he said, repeating himself.

I doubted if there ever was any gold. A trace maybe; enough to get folks excited for a summer. Winter would change all that.

"Got any family?" I asked him.

He shook his head no. I nodded in understanding.

"Got any place you want to go? Want to cross the river?"

He shook his head. "Left the cat," he said. "Left the pigeons. No horses to feed."

"They'll get along," I said. "But you..., you might want to cross the river, maybe get yourself into Kane, get something in your belly. Old lady Neely will give you a place to sleep, you ask her." I paused trying not to be impatient. "Listen Old Timer, the ferryman--he's awaitin'. Do you want help gettin' across? I could give you a hand."

The old man started to rise but his legs were unsteady and began to give way. He got mostly up before he sat back down, breathing out as he did, air rattling from his lungs. He coughed like he was choking, then for a moment was silent. "No," he finally said, "I'll stay here. I'll not be going anywhere. Not tonight. I think this is it. I ain't goin' anywheres."

I watched the ferryman rise from his stool, step outside his shack with the cup still in his hand. He was looking at the herd of sheep across the river and then glanced at me to see if I would be wanting his services. I waved my hand at him letting him know I was coming. I didn't want to swim the river with the cool of evening coming on. It was still dropping down close to freezing during the night. I reckon the damn dog didn't want to swim either but I didn't know. Like I said, he was notional.

I glanced at the old man sitting on the log, slouched over. "Suit yourself," I said. "Maybe tomorrow then."

I mounted.

"Maybe tomorrow," the old man repeated absently. "Left the cat and the pigeons," he said slowly. "Gold petered out."

I nudged the bay forward. There was nothing I could do. There were no tomorrows for the old man. The only thing he had left was a lot of yesterdays, and a cat who hadn't eaten, living in an empty barn with a pack rat or two and an attic full of starving pigeons. I made sure Smith saw me coming. He lifted his empty cup in recognition.

The dog was on my heels as I rode the bay onto the ferry and dismounted.

Big Horn River Ferry at Kane

CHAPTER 2

SHEEP FLOATING IN AIR

John Smith's ferry and the Indian Tree that stood across the county road from his homestead were one mile from the front door to Riley Kane's U.S. Post Office in Kane, Wyoming. Give or take a foot or two, and depending on where you happened to be standing. The town of Lovell twelve miles further west is one hundred sixty-three feet higher in elevation than John Smith's ferry on the Big Horn River. This altitude factor gave the "up there" folks in Lovell a sense of superiority to those "down there" folks, living in Kane. Not that it mattered much to the folks in Kane, but folks always need something that sets them apart from everyone else.

Facts are facts and the fact was that when the folks in Lovell got up in the morning, drank their morning coffee, ate some fried potatoes and a baking soda biscuit, their horses would have to walk downhill twelve miles to get to Kane. Certainly they were higher up. Fact was also that every morning the sun came up over Lovell first and set on Kane last. The mountain saw to that. And that is the way it was and the way it had always been. So folks said when they needed something to brag about as they sipped their hot coffee and saddled their ornery, blockheaded horses.

The locomotive engineer for the Chicago, Burlington and Quincy Railroad knew that Lovell was higher than Kane. The Shoshone River which ran between both settlements was proof of that. He also knew that the railroad grade on the south side of Kane was gentle and that the next town, Greybull, was uphill forty miles. Greybull was significant to the railroad because of its roundtable, its section yards, engine repair shops, and its housing for the gandy dancers it employed. Greybull was also the engineer's end of line. It was where he lived when he wasn't monitoring the throttle, brakes, and pressure gauges of the big, black locomotive 2460.

On the run to Greybull from Billings the engineer slowed down at Lovell for several reasons. One: it was a rail stop, a place to unload freight if freight was the make up of the train. It was also a place for passengers to get on and off, or sit tight waiting if the engine was pulling passenger cars. Two: if he was hauling freight, slowing down was a courtesy to those high-browed folks and their dogs that lived in Lovell. It gave those mutts the opportunity to chase trains and catch them if they felt so inclined. Not many did. Besides a slow train makes less racket as one does moving fast with the engineer laying on the horn. He wasn't supposed to do that except before a crossing. There were three crossings in Lovell starting just before he crossed the railroad bridge over the Shoshone a mile west of the Lovell town limits.

After years of making the Billings-Greybull run, the engineer had established certain customs. A

12

mile east of Lovell he would lean back in his chair perched high above the rails. He'd glance back and watch for the brakeman to wave the red lantern, giving him the "go ahead" and "all clear" sign. Once he saw the lantern, he'd pull halfway down on the throttle and lock it in place. The engine would start to hum as it began to labor under a new head of steam, driving the iron wheels down the iron tracks. Just outside Lovell the engineer always craved speed. However, his first concern after locking the throttle down in a new setting was the curve in the track a mile before reaching Kane. That half-mile curve changed the direction of the tracks from east to due south. After the turn he'd be following the Big Horn River all the way to Greybull.

There were two rail crossings on that curve in the tracks. One led east to the Big Horn River, the mountain and John Smith's ferry. One led north to Iona and the old railroad bridge that spanned the Shoshone. The old bridge hadn't seen a train in some time and now was used for wagons, an occasional horse back rider, and foot traffic. Its sole purpose was allowing folks to cross the Shoshone river without getting wet. The two rail crossings were less than two hundred yards apart on either end of the bend in the tracks.

His second concern (if he were to think about it, which he didn't) was the incidental fact that he didn't want to be in such a hurry that speed would cause the train to leave the tracks rounding that corner.

13

What he did want was sufficient speed to push the engine and forty-six cars uphill from Kane for as far as he could without slowing down. Not that he could make Greybull without having to adjust the throttle. He couldn't. Greybull was forty miles away. But he could make Sheep Mountain Canyon. He could get Engine 2460 past Beaver Flat and the limestone caves before the engine began to labor, slowing down. Speed would save fuel, coal, and steam. Not that he thought much about that either.

After all, the Chicago, Burlington and Quincy had plenty of coal. It was a railroad for heaven's sakes. He didn't say that. He said other things instead.

For a moment, he thought about these factors before disregarding them, then hunkered down in his chair with his thermos of hot coffee and his empty cup. Bottom line: he wanted to get home, he wanted to get off that train, kiss his wife, and find his fishing pole. The engineer's home was in Greybull, Wyoming just three blocks east of the section house. That's what he wanted. Taking a breath, he glanced at the throttle and wondered if he dared pull it down a quarter of an inch more. No, he answered, he'd leave it where it was for at least another mile. Maybe he'd wait until reaching the Sunlight Flat, then he'd advance the throttle. There was a smile on his whiskered face.

In an hour I'll be home, he thought. *Maybe less. I need speed.*

He glanced at the throttle a second time and shook his head. The fireman noted the small gesture.

Just east of Lovell the engineer blew the whistle, holding the lever down. Across Lovell town, before the hill and just below the canal, Mr. Johnson turned in his sleep, wakened just long enough to know he didn't want to be awake.

Damn train, anyway.

Somewhere on Third Street a dog barked like someone had kicked him hard. Mrs. Richardson's rooster crowed. The whistle blast echoed along the ridges north of the Shoshone river and grew silent. Except for the rooster, the town returned to some semblance of quiet. Releasing the whistle rope, the engineer filled his cup, watching the steam rise from its contents, then he stared down the advancing track.

Sunlight Flat...I'll adjust that throttle, he thought.

It was April. Sheep herds in Kane were not happenstance. Up country the sheep had eaten what there was to eat. There was no more. So in April they sought more and grass was greening on the east side of the river. John Smith's ferry was the only way to cross it.

Old man Fred O'Conner had his band of Columbia ewes up and moving at first light. There was considerable commotion as three hundred ewes located their lambs and the dogs started them circling. Nothing grew on the badlands west of Kane. Not even in the Spring. Bentonite doesn't support much foliage. He couldn't keep sheep on the barren slopes; not for long. Moving wasn't the problem. Hungry sheep move quickly and in a dozen different directions: hence, the need for dogs. Besides, he wanted to be at the ferry early, first in line, waiting for John Smith to get his feet out from under the breakfast table. Not the other way around. No time to dillydally. O'Conner could eat once the band was across the Horn and moving toward new grass on Low Mountain.

The Irishman drove the band north out of the badlands, then east down the county road 14A, toward the big river. The dogs monitored the stragglers, keeping the sheep together. Fred rode a sorrel saddle horse, giving his dogs instructions as needed. Every once in a while he'd take a sip from the dark-green bottle he kept in his inside coat pocket. On his left was the barbed wire fence that keep livestock off the Chicago, Burlington and Quincy Railroad and right of way. The tracks were fenced to the first crossing, but not after. Folks needed to get across the tracks. Barbed wire just got in the way.

O'Conner turned in the saddle and looked up-track, west toward Lovell. There was nothing on the rails this morning; nothing that he could see or hear. He'd made good time. The railroad crossing leading to the Big Horn River was several hundred yards ahead of the leaders. It was a perfect morning. The band was moving quickly down the gravel road to the tracks and passed the two room school building up on the hill on his left.

Outside of Lovell nine and one half miles east was the Sunlight Flat. Ever since leaving the settlement the engine speed had been steadily increasing. After all, it was downhill. The engineer glanced at the speed indicator and nodded his head at the fireman.

"Can you give me a little more?" he asked. "I'll be needing it when we turn the corner."

The fireman, a short, stubby fellow wearing a blue, faded shirt, a sack of Bull Durham in the left pocket, nodded his head. "No problem," he said. "You in some sort of hurry?"

"Not really," the engineer replied and smiled. "Don't wanna slow down. That's what I don't wanna do."

"Got a girl? Seems like you got a girl."

"Got three. My wife, Mildred Louise, and two daughters. Got a son, too. The oldest, she's turning seventeen today. Havin' a celebration. And I'm gonna go fishing as soon as I eat cake and drink a little lemonade."

"Don't know if I'd be likin' that combination. Not from the sound of it."

The fireman fed the firebox more coal. Both men stared at the boiler pressure gauge. The fireman nodded. "You got pressure if you want to release some steam, push her a bit."

The engineer nodded, satisfied. He had her right where she needed to be to make the curve. In forty-six minutes he'd be home. Damn. That sounded good.

Three minutes passed. The engineer turned and spoke to the fireman, "Coffee?" he asked.

17

The fireman was staring past the engineer through the front windshield. He answered in a whisper. "Jesus," he said.

"What?" The engineer paused, unsure if the fireman understood. "I said, do you want some coffee? It's still hot. Well, it's warm." The engineer looked at him. The fireman's jaw opened, it moved, but he didn't or couldn't say anything. Nothing came out.

The engineer turned to see what had the fireman's attention. First he saw a man on a saddle horse, rising up in the stirrups, waving his arms frantically. In an automatic response the engineer started to raise his hand to acknowledge the greeting, but then he saw the three hundred sheep and as many lambs. They all seemed to be standing on the track looking right at him.

The mind plays tricks on a man at times. The engineer actually thought of braking, but there was no use in that. He had tons upon tons of steel pushing him. He couldn't stop if he wanted to. He couldn't slow down if he wanted to. Already he was turning south. Certainly he did want to slow her down but saw no use in it. No purpose.

In that fraction of a second, with time standing still, the engineer reached his hand for the whistle lever and pulled it down. With the other, he grabbed the throttle and advanced it, immediately feeling the pent up steam surge into the pistons that drove the iron wheels.

This train she ain't slowin' down, he thought. *Gotta make Greybull sometime today.*

18

The cowcatcher traveling at sixty-eight miles per hour hit the first ewe. It flew up in the morning air eighteen feet and fell past the locomotive's open window, turning and twisting as it dropped. Then the train hit the band. Sheep flew through the air, flying every which way, like driving hail caught in the wind. Others folded under the wheels and track. The engine didn't feel the impact. There wasn't a thump or a bump.

The fireman stood leaning against the side window looking back down the track. "Jesus," he said again. "Frank, you gotta see this. They're jumping under the wheels! It's like they are being sucked under. I'll be damned. I ain't never seen the like!" He turned to look at the engineer. "You gonna stop?" he asked. "What...?"

The fireman watched the engineer advance the throttle and knew the answer.

Didn't much matter, he thought. *The train would be halfway to Greybull before they could slow her down. Might as well take her on home.*

He looked back through the open window at the racing freight cars, watching the wheels slice through sheep. All around him rose the noise of the engine powering up, the rattling freight cars beating out a syncopated rhythm against the rails. Clack, clack, clack, clickity-clack. On the exterior flanks of the herd the dogs were racing back and forth, barking, keeping the sheep pressed up against the track and the rolling freight cars. That was their training. That is what they did.

Just as suddenly the tail end of the train was among the frantic, spinning, milling sheep, then through the herd and gone. The whistle blared its warning to all that would listen, the echo bouncing off the grey hills again and again. It seemed a little late.

The whistle stopped screaming. Except for the bleating of wounded and dying sheep and the barking of dogs, silence reigned.

The sheep herder watched the dark red caboose moving up the track, then he stared at the mountain then at the cottonwood trees that lined the river bottom. He thought aloud to himself,

"John Smith, you takes your time with your morning cup. I'll be a little longer, I expect. No use hurryin' to hurry on my account. 'Cause you gots plenty of time a waitin' on me a waitin' on a train that I sure as hell didn't wait for."

The sorrel's ears were twitching back and forth listening to the rider speak. The old man laughed ,then yelled angrily at his dogs. He had them back off from what was left of the noble three hundred. Those that were alive had moved or were crossing the bloodied tracks and were gathering along the canal bank drinking and browsing on greasewood and sagebrush as if nothing had happened. Several had gone back to the railroad tracks looking for their lambs.

At least them damn dogs can hear me now, he thought

He took another nip from his green bottle and wondered if the Chicago, Burlington and Quincy would pay for the sheep they'd killed. He doubted that would be his fortune then nudged the sorrel forward, intent on counting the dead before he pushed the remaining herd down the dirt road to the river.

CHAPTER 3

SHOSHONE COLD AND DEEP

Preface

*Unlike the Big Horn the Shoshone runs fast.
When March dies and April arrives it brings the first
warm winds of spring. The glacial snows of Sylvan
Pass begin to melt as they have for thousands upon
thousands of years. Each drop, each trickle, each
gush of snow melt flows down the steep slopes and
becomes the head water of the Shoshone. Each mile
the Shoshone is augmented with the flood waters of
creek after creek and those from the Thoroughfare
and from each gully and canyon and tributary
thereafter. She grows and grows until her waters
cascade through the canyon west of Cody then out
into the Basin. Thus in the spring the Shoshone
invariably runs high and deep. Because of the drop
in elevation of several thousand feet she runs fast.*

*From its beginnings the Shoshone throws
itself against rock and boulder, churning itself white,
building itself a frothy foam, beating rocks into sand.
In the spring she expands her borders tearing
cottonwoods away by their roots, moving rock and
sediment at will, changing channels, moving like a
whip, straightening the bend, bending the straight,
ever on the move, roaring through white water*

rapids. Nothing stops the river as she makes her mad dash to the Big Horn.

The Shoshone was ice water from the first drop to the last,, its mother the deep snows of winter that clung to the sides of Sylvan Pass. On the fly, from headwater to end, she is seventy miles, give or take. Every mile downhill. Later, after the dam was built all that she had been disappeared and was diverted away into lost channels of irrigation water and the edge of irrelevancy.

The Shoshone was feared before she was plugged, dammed, and her water diverted into a dozen canals and sent out on the benches of Cody and Powell to irrigate beans, beets and sunflowers. Before, she had a flood plain that actually flooded. Afterwards, she was barely a whisper. The fresh cut banks crumbled; the cottonwood grew large and formidable, sinking their roots deep into the river bed unconcerned with the river that was. There were times afterwards when a cloudburst beat up the McCullough Peaks and once again nothing could stop her. Sometimes after days on days of rain she began to remember who she had been. Sometimes she even thought about expanding beyond her banks. But not like before, not running a half mile out from the river bed as she had once done, before man, before barrels of concrete and Bill Cody.

In 1927 Babe Ruth hit 60 home runs. Big, rotund and silent Calvin Coolidge was President. In early May of that year the Shoshone river wasn't running high, nor was it running yellow. After all, since 1910 she had had a concrete dam to contend with as well as diversion canals. Late May, she changed and became a little ornery; her natural self, invigorated by rain and more rain that fell above Clark, Cody and Ralston.

Red, riding a dun gilding, had left his mother's home on the Kane Flat and was looking to get to the Iona side of the river and the distant bank of the Stinking Water. At river's edge he sat the dun and studied the rushing water. It was choppy white, grey with silt.

Maybe today ain't a good time, he thought. *But...when it came to fording an angry river what day was good?*

Pulling his hat down around his ears, Red pushed the reluctant dun into the edge waters of the river. The dun walked gingerly as if the smooth rock hurt its feet. The water was to his knees. Fifteen feet later his belly was wet. The north bank looked farther away than Red first imagined. Still the horse's feet found a tenuous purchase on the rocky bottom. He could feel the horses uncertainty in the hesitant manner in which the dun placed his feet. Suddenly the dun was swimming and the bottom was simply gone. The surging current was rolling up Red's pant leg filling his boots, splashing onto his pockets. Even the saddle seat was wet. Horse and rider were swept downstream.

Maybe it was the swiftness of the current. Maybe the horse touched the river bed for an instant, the bottom giving away. Maybe his horse was struck by a floating log. Whatever the cause, the dun suddenly rolled to his left side dumping Red into the ice water. Upside down, sideways Red tried to jump free from the horse, his boot momentarily caught in the stirrup, knee against the saddle shoulder. Rolling, spinning, flipping, his sense of up was gone. His right hand gripped the saddle horn. His foot hit rock bottom. There was no air to breathe. No way to see. The horse rolled then righted itself. In the depths Red grabbed for rock, found one and held on, lost his grip, grabbed another, clinging to the bottom. Something struck his legs and was gone. What? Dare he turn loose? He wondered where his horse was, where its hooves were. The rushing current seemed to turn him, pulling his body parallel to the river bottom, twisting it. Red held on it seemed like forever, until his lungs felt like they were exploding, crying for respite.

A second passed.

Where was his horse? About to kick him in the head? He pulled himself closer to the rock he'd siezed, closer to his chest and chin. The strong current, the swiftly moving water seemingly pulled him deeper. His head hit a rock; it must have been a rock for sparks flew inside his head like sparklers. He felt himself slipping, suddenly the bottom fell away. Then rolling, his body rose to meet him in a rush. Instinctively, he grabbed for another boulder, hoping to stay low. The horse's thrashing, egg beater hooves churned above him. He clutched at a rock, straining against the current. In the dark waters he hung on. It seemed like split seconds. Not knowing if he was clear of the horse, his uncertainty was compounded.

Another second passed.

He tried to push off and up with his feet. Something happened...he didn't know what. The water pulled him, rolled him. He tried to find the top but it felt like the bottom. Ears and mouth were full of water. Rocks scraped his knees. Again he pushed away from the rocky bottom.

Another second passed.

After what seemed like minutes his face broke the surface. He gasped, sucking air into his tortured lungs. The current twisted him about, rolling his torso. The north bank loomed up fast. Before his blinking eyes were tree roots and rock imbedded in dirt and then it was gone and he was under water again. The current spinning him.

Another second passed.

By some miracle he was shoved into a more shallow part of the river, his feet found the rock bottom, then sand. He started to struggle toward shore gasping for air, sucking it into his tortured lungs.

One hundred yards below him the dun had reached safety on the north shore, belly-dragging its saddle. Red, all five foot six inches of him, started swimming. In spite of his efforts, it was some time before he, too, got himself to dry land.

Once there he couldn't just collapse. He wanted to. He'd have liked to. Walking wasn't a good idea either. He had to chase the dun, weighed down by water sloshing in his boots, wet clothes clinging to his skin, and no hat. If he didn't hurry he'd have nothing to eat; he'd be walking. The horse wasn't waiting for another ice water bath. Half a mile farther downstream Red caught up to him. That was as far as Red traveled that Tuesday. He'd barely made two miles but two miles was enough. Today wasn't a good time to go on. Besides he had to look for his hat, dry his clothes, warm his cramping leg muscles and thank the river god he wasn't dead.

CHAPTER 4

CATTLE ON ICE

Preface

The Big Horn froze over in winter. It had always been so. Sometimes the ice would form sixteen inches thick, thicker if the cold lasted longer. It often did. In the early days of Wyoming history its water ran clear. A man looking down from his saddle horse, his horse swimming and his boots filling with water, could see the bottom easily. The old killer was the home for catfish, river trout, bull heads and sunken logs. The Horn's serpentine body stretched from Wind River to the Narrows. A little over a hundred miles. After the Narrows, she became a canyon river all the way to old Fort Smith or what was left of it.

Never was there a year when the river didn't claim some poor soul who, as it turned out, wasn't as good of a swimmer as he thought he was. Once the river took him seldom did she give him back. His body, invariably, would be lost downstream in the canyon never to be seen again. That's the way it was. If the river took him, the river kept him and there'd be nothing to bury in the Iona cemetery. Not being buried in Iona was not a loss. That excuse for a "final resting place" was a dull rock garden located on the south side of a rocky hill. Nothing grew there except sage brush, greasewood, cheat grass and the number of wooden markers. Real bunch grass wouldn't live there. Invariably the wooden markers would weather, rot and disappear. Later, the pine caskets would cave in, leaving depressions about a foot deep, shallow dimples on a gravel knoll. Thus, at least in Iona, even the dead were lost in time. The gossip had it that there are folks buried there that didn't know they were dead. No one told them for fear they'd get up and move.

During the cold months the river would freeze thick but not solid clear though. It wasn't that cold. Men would come in wagons, saw holes in her and pull out blocks of ice, hauling them away. The ice was so thick that it supported men and their wagons loaded with ice blocks pulled by teams of horses. There were no spectators. If you weren't working, you weren't there. The blocks of ice once extracted were stored in log buildings called ice houses. The ice blocks were stacked on top of each other. Each block was covered in sawdust to keep it free from its neighbor. Otherwise they'd freeze together and become one big unusable block of ice ten feet high and twenty feet long.

In the heat of summer the ice would be used to cool ice boxes and refrigerate fresh milk, butter and lemonade if you were lucky enough to have lemons and a sack of sugar. If the ice house was well-built, it'd preserve the ice until late in the summer. Neighbors would know if you were any good at ice house construction if they drank ice *water in September. The trick was the thickness of the logs. Insulation helped.*

Come spring the snow would start to melt and the river water would rise and with it the sheet of ice that covered it. Tension would grow in the center, increasing hourly. The water would get deeper and deeper until suddenly, without warning, the blanket of ice would pop loose, breaking up into giant sheets all the way from Sheep Canyon to the Narrows. It sounded like cannons firing in celebration of the Fourth of July.

The cracked and broken ice sheets would drift downstream and jam into the Narrows, plugging the flow of water, momentarily backing the river up until she broke loose again with a thunderous roar. Getting across the river in late March, first of April was a dangerous proposition few wanted to undertake. Mostly folks didn't. Waiting a couple of weeks wouldn't kill you. Not waiting . . .well that might.

The Horn was broad, two hundred plus feet, enough that an island formed with river water from both the Horn and Shoshone flowing on both sides. In the spring and summer the island grass grew thick amidst the young cottonwood trees.

On the north end resided an old lady skunk. Every year she'd have a brood of kittens and every year those kittens would escape to the mainland. How she got pregnant was a mystery, as was why she stayed on the island. She didn't have to and she didn't have much company. It was an Agatha Christie mystery.

She arrived on a cottonwood log that she caught floating down the middle of the Shoshone River. She was clinging to it when the Shoshone joined with the Big Horn. As luck would have it the log lodged itself on the island's southern tip. Saved by good fortune and serendipity, the skunk stepped primly off, soaked to the skin, and shook herself. She immediately moved to the north end to set up her puzzling housekeeping.

The Southern end of the island, and the reason the skunk didn't stay there long, was the residence of an old bull badger. He got there by walking across on ice sometime during the cool months of the year. Once he arrived he stayed, living in a labyrinth of dens built under a large rotting cottonwood log. The log was a smorgasbord of grubs, earthworms and sweetness, it once being a hive for wild honey bees. It was an easy decision for the old badger; living close to the restaurant had its benefits. Once he happened on this culinary good fortune he never left. Besides, no one bothered him. His solitary life rarely exposed his ill temper.

Lee and Rose Hoffman used the island grass in the summer and fall to feed their cows. Whether they owned the island was debatable. Islands grow, shrink and move continually, as do the rivers that give them life and cause them to appear and, conversely, disappear. After the river froze in early winter, they'd wait for the ice to thicken, then they

31

spread loose hay across the ice in "close together" bunches. The hungry cows would follow the sweet alfalfa hay across the ice to the island. Once on the island they stayed, liking the lush forage, not liking the unsure slippery feel of ice. Out in the middle of the river the island feed was convenient and the grass thick. And his cows? Well, Lee knew where they were without having to string barbed wire and dig fence post holes to keep them where he wanted. "Why not?" Lee would answer when asked about the practice. "I know where they are. They're gaining weight. And they're happy. The perfect arrangement." He brought them back home when they started calving in mid-February.

In February of what was the last island year, sometime toward the beginning of the calving season, Rose and Lee laid fresh hay across the channel ice between island and mainland. Thus they enticed the forty-three head of cows, three yearling bulls, and twenty yearling heifers back across the ice to the hay fields. It was a matter of ease. It was easier to walk out to the corral to check on cows about to give birth than it was to saddle a horse and ride to the island for the same purpose. It seemed like the thing to do. They'd done it many times for exactly the same reason. Why change?

But change did come. It always does. She came with a cold wind blowing up river driving dried cottonwood leaves across the ice. The skies were grey and Low Mountain was hidden in fog. The hay bait was distributed across the channel. Out on the ice, cows were moving quickly from one bunch to the next, moving steadily, walking across the ice toward the promise of waiting hay fields. Inevitably, some ran back not liking what they found, remembering instead what they'd left behind. Others kept going, following the hay bait in this western version of "Hansel and Gretel." On the shore line Rose was standing in the back of her Ford pickup truck counting cows as they came across. She'd gotten to six. Number seven was on her lips.

There came a loud pop of ice breaking that seemed to shake the very ground. Rose could feel the shudder from where she was perched in the back of the Ford high above the river. Lee was sitting on his sorrel saddle horse beside the Ford. Both looked east across the ice toward the island. The cows' heads came up from their flakes of hay, their jaws moving, unsure, their legs suddenly unstable. Several turned and began to run back from whence they came. Others still followed the leaders, arriving almost to the west river bank. Weight was redistributed across the ice shelf. To Lee's amazement the northern portion of the ice sheet began to tilt upward, rising slowly above the river like the bow of the stricken Titanic. Cows were bawling as they fought to maintain their balance. Several head that had reached the west shore turned back at the sudden commotion, confused as to whether to go or stay.

Rose stepped back in the bed of the Ford pickup her mouth open, astonished.

On the ice several head dropped into the cold, swirling water, their bodies rolling as they took the plunge and started swimming frantically.

Another sheet of thick ice broke loose. Twenty head dropped into the current, followed by more and more, then all. The river pulled the bobbing, frantic cows northward, downstream. One by one they disappeared, pulled under the unbroken remaining ice shelf. In less then thirty seconds they were gone. All of them. Four of the six head that had made it ashore jumped back into the river and shortly disappeared under the ice with the rest. It was quiet except for the gurgling river water and a magpie.

Rose, seeing the last cow carried beneath the ice, bent over herself as if in pain and horror. Her foot slipped on the slick, cold metal of the tailgate. She toppled backwards, her arms flailing, striking the frozen ground hard, landing across a broken branch, and a large rock. Pain shot up her back. Bones in her lower spine broke, leaving her right leg numb and useless. Her scream split the air. Lee's head snapped around, seeing her writhing in a heap on the ground. He jumped off the sorrel and ran to her.

At her side, Lee was left standing in devastating silence, alone, his wife whimpering in pain at his feet. From far south he could hear the freight train blowing its whistle as it emerged from Sheep Canyon: two blasts followed by one long. The code signified nothing to Lee. He was busy trying to figure out how to get Rose into the cab of the Ford truck with her fighting his every attempt to move her.

Cutting Ice Blocks on the Big Horn River

Lee's Icy Corrals on the Big Horn

CHAPTER 5

WOMAN STANDING IN ICE WATER

Low Mountain is a barometer of sorts. In the winter the storms roll in from the west and the clouds hang low on her rock-barren slopes. It is then the scrub juniper and cottonwood disappear and vanish in the cold haze. Sometimes the clouds hang so low she can't be seen at all. Sometimes winter takes a notion to explain how she won't be taken for granted any longer, how you'd better bring a good heavy coat because she ain't listening to any whining. "No," the mountain says, "Not any more; not now." That's when she gets serious and the thermometer bellies out at forty below. That's when it's God-awful cold and Low Mountain disappears altogether. Yes, sometimes she's a barometer, a harbinger of how Hell is going to feel to those not given to fire, but think ice will, indeed, suffice.

Pete Gervay hadn't returned. Since his leaving it had been twenty-four hours. Elizabeth was well aware of the time. The sun had gone down and come up and Pete wasn't there. It was a simple conclusion. She waited, watching. Sometimes she could barely see that round ball of fire; its tracks passing through grey clouds: a hazy circle of moving light. In the fog-grey it became more of a memory than a reality. Pete had left yesterday morning to hunt deer along Porcupine Creek but he failed to return in the evening. "I'll be getting some fresh meat," he said, turning his back away from her, a Winchester rifle slung over his shoulder. His not returning worried her because he always returned. Not once since they were married had she slept alone. That first time was yesterday. Now she was alone on Little Mountain with a growing belly and Pike the Border Collie. It was beginning to feel like snow. There was a dry crispness in the air that hadn't been there before. A breeze picked up. It felt colder. It smelled colder. It was colder. She pulled the cabin door shut and turned to the iron cook stove.

She was fortunate, always a sound sleeper. Not even Pete's ragged snoring kept her awake. Lately she woke when the baby started kicking. It kicked her mostly after she laid down or when she sat down at the kitchen table to rest. She wondered exactly how long she'd been pregnant. *At least seven months,* she thought. *Probably longer. It had to be at least that long.* Sometimes during the night she'd wake Pete, take his hand and place it on her extended belly so he could feel the baby kicking. He'd smile in the dark and hold her close. She liked that. But now there was no Pete, no arms holding her, no whiskers scratching her cheek. With or without him the nights seemed longer.

Stop it, she thought. *It's only been twenty four hours. Not long.* She repeated those instructions to herself again and again. Pete would know what to do wherever he was. If it snowed, if the wind became too difficult, he'd hole up. He'd build a fire and keep warm. He'd just wait for the storm to blow over. That's what he'd do. Storms always blow over. He'd be smart because he was smart. Right now he was probably sitting in front of a warm fire, his back against a rock wall, waiting, being smart, keeping the cold away from his shoulders, the wind out of his hair. Many times he'd said to her, "You find yourself in trouble: Think. Just stop and think. You'll be all right."

Elizabeth Gervay thought about her husband being in trouble, if he were in trouble. *He'll stop. He'll think. He'll be all right. So I need to do what I always do,* she told herself. *I need to think. I need to fix breakfast. I need to eat. I need to be patient and Pete will be here before I know it. He'll know what to do. Surely. I'll take a nap. That way the waiting will seem like I'm not waiting at all. I'll wake up and he'll be here.*

She waited. She dozed. She awoke. But Pete hadn't returned. He wasn't there.

There was the dog. Pike kept her company, watching her. She looked at him, waiting. "At least there's you. Huh? Do ya want a bone? I'll get you one. What did you do with the one I gave you yesterday? You gnaw it to a sliver? Did you?" Pike whined in response, moving from one side of the table to the other.

Mid-morning of the second day the wind rose. She stepped outside to get more wood for the wood box. Pike followed her, sniffing at the wind. Her skirts were billowing about her legs as she fought with the axe. South, below the cabin, grey clouds shrouded Devil's Canyon in a mist. It hid Medicine Mountain under a thick blanket. Snow was in the air. She could feel it, the sharp, dry crispness of it. Occasionally she could see a few flakes driven by the wind, passing by in a rush.

Once she had enough chopped wood to fill the wood box she brought the double bladed axe inside with Pike following behind her. Sitting at the table with ever growing impatience, she waited, listening to the wind, listening to her heartbeat in the silence of the four walls. Repeatedly she stood up, walked to the window to peer out. Pete had placed that window in the south side of the cabin so she could see down the canyon while she washed dishes. It was small but it was her window. She stared through it at drifting snow. Pike whined, lying down on the braided rug in front of the cook stove.

Cold seeped into everything. By mid-day she found it difficult to see out through the window glass. Ice had gathered along the edges and was creeping to the middle. By mid-afternoon the glass was opaque, a solid sheet of ice. The cabin was becoming a tomb. It felt as if she was breathing inside a large wooden box with no opening, the top closing in on her. Except for the wind and Pike, a suffocating silence surrounded her.

She chided herself for entertaining her fears, for letting her mind play tricks and conjuring up so many horrible things. In the quiet she imagined Pete lost, unable to find his way, maybe falling into a crevice. Maybe he couldn't get out, snow piling on top of him, holding him down. Maybe wolves had attacked him, tearing him apart, ripping his arms off, gnawing his bones. Maybe he'd broken through the ice, falling into the cold waters of Porcupine Creek. Maybe he'd lost his matches; maybe they were wet; maybe the wind blew his fire out. Maybe he had no wood to burn. Maybe he broke his leg, his arm. Maybe he'd fallen to his death from the canyon rim. It could happen. In the ground fog, one step and he'd be tumbling a thousand feet and no one would know.

Fix supper, she told herself. *Feed the dog. Just get hold of yourself. You foolish girl. Pete will come. Stop thinking. Just stop thinking.*

That's what she told herself but she didn't think she could. And she didn't. Instead she jumped at every sound, hoping that at any minute he'd come through the door in a flurry of snow, laughing at her.

He'd say, "Had you worried, Liz? No problems, lady. What's a little snow? Got a big buck hanging in the shed. What's that on your cheeks? Tears? You been crying? Come here, girl. Everything is all right. We're in the pink. Got fresh venison to eat. Wood to burn. It's snowing? It's cold? Don't matter now. We're ready."

Evening came and went and still no Pete.

Late evening of the third day she ate potatoes she'd boiled along with the last of the venison roast. They were warm when she started them boiling in the pot; hot, even. Within minutes, seconds, they were cold on the tin plate. She fed some to Pike. He didn't seem to mind hot or cold.

In the growing darkness she no longer tried to convince herself that Pete was returning; that all would be well just as soon as he came in from the cold. She reminded herself that in all probability he'd holed up until the storm blew over. *It surely hadn't blown over! If anything it had picked up intensity.* She remembered it hadn't been storming when he was supposed to have returned. That small factor bothered her, nagging at her emotional sensibilities, wearing at her desire to be reasonable. She lit the oil lamp using one match. *He'll need a light to find his way*, she thought. *If he can find his way in this soup. If he is alive, in one piece. There were so many ifs.*

Pike stood up, walked to the door and scratched it.

"What boy? What do you want? Hear something?"

The dog looked at her, whined.

"You want out?"

She let him out only to have him return a short time later, scratching at the door to be allowed in.

She opened the door. Stared outside and saw no one but the dog.

In the muted light she listened to the wind howling about the eaves. *He'll use common sense*, she told herself for the hundredth time. *So should I. If he doesn't come before nightfall, I'll bank the fire and lie down under the heavy blankets. Keep myself warm. I'll wait. The storm has to break soon. It can't last forever. Neither can I*, she thought. *Neither can I.*

Pete didn't come.

The third night she crawled under the blankets, telling herself to expect him at any moment. For the third night she slept fitfully. She dozed. The wind howling around the eaves woke her. She listened, dozed again. When she woke the third time she lay awake thinking the thumping she heard might be Pete. But it was just the wind banging limbs against the cabin wall, branches brushing against the roof. Outside it was pitch black. Moon and stars were hidden. The room cooled quickly even though the stove burned red.

Soon the heat will be gone, she thought. *It will be freezing in here.*

Unconsciously she felt across the bed. There was no Pete. She chided herself because she knew he wasn't there before her fingers stretched in vain across the bedding to the very edge. There was no Pete.

Silly girl, she thought

The baby kicked. She groaned, rubbing her belly.

Not now, she thought. *Be patient, little one. Your Daddy is coming home. He always comes home. Always.*

She dozed again and awoke, having no idea how long she slept. It could have been ten minutes or ten hours or two days. Pike wanted out. She got up and opened the door for him. In the dark she found herself waiting for sunrise, wishing for it, praying for it. It came, finally, but it seemed a very long time coming. All the while the wind howled, moaning, whispering, bending branch and twig. The baby didn't stop kicking.

She remembered thinking *Oh my God, my God. Please, please help me.* Then there was nothing but the cold.

He must have heard her for when she awoke the room was light enough to see. She arose tired and started a fire in the stove. It took five blue tipped Diamond matches.

Not good, she thought. *I'll have to start a lot of fires. Except I can't. The matches won't last. The wood won't last. The food won't last. There will be no water unless I melt snow. I'll have to,* she thought. *I have no choice.*

No, silly girl, I have food. There's half a deer hanging in the lean-to. I have flour. I have sugar. I have molasses and potatoes and I have wood. I just have to go outside to get it. I'll have to chop it; break it up some so it'll fit in the stove. I can do that inside.

How long can I last without Pete? Oh my God. He's really not coming? Something terrible has happened. It has. I just know it. And I'm so pregnant, so very pregnant. I could be snowed in for weeks and months. Oh my God, my God. She thought. *It must be thirty, forty below outside! Who could possibly survive in that cold?* She heard Pike scratching at the door.

She answered her question out loud. "No one," she said. The sound of her voice was hollow in her ears, flat, dying instantly.

The snow must have drifted up around the walls, maybe on the roof, she thought. *It is absorbing sound.*

She went to the door, released the latch and pushed on it. The door didn't move. She pushed again and again without results. It felt as if snow had drifted in behind it. She went to the window. It was a white sheet of ice. She could hear Pike scratching.

I'm trapped. I can't get out of my own house.

Hopelessness washed over her. She lit the lamp and sat on the edge of the bed staring at the door. Tears welled up in her eyes. The baby started kicking, reminding her of the life growing inside her.

Buck up, girl, she thought. *It isn't over and we ain't dead.*

Elizabeth laid down and pulled the covers over her head. Her stomach growled, reminding her she hadn't eaten breakfast. She hadn't even fixed breakfast. She slept. When she woke the fire was out and she remembered Pike.

What am I going to do about you, dog? she thought. *About me?*

Sitting on the edge of the bed in the dim light, she noticed something peculiar about the door. Something she hadn't noticed before. Ice had formed along the top of the door frame, melted when she started the fire, and ran down the boards to the floor where it had re-frozen on the dirt floor.

Hey, girl, it might not be snow drifting behind the door. It might be frozen shut. It might be ice.

She found comfort in the thought. Somewhere she'd put the axe, having brought it inside when she filled the wood box. As silly as it had seemed she brought it inside because she didn't want to have to look for it in a snowdrift.

This silly girl is smart for once. Really smart. Elizabeth smiled. The baby kicked. *No, indeed. We ain't dead. Not yet. And we ain't got to look for the axe.*

She spent the morning chipping the ice away from the door, listening to Pike. She was so relieved when the door opened even a little. Pike crawled in through the small space. It wasn't just the ice. There was snow behind it also. But it opened a little giving her a glimmer of hope and a little light on a dark day. Pike looked up at her.

"What do you want?" she said. "It's your fault. You should have stayed inside. Stupid dog."

Elizabeth's days merged one into another and another and another and another. In dark hours, in shade and shadow, in drifting snow and wind, she simply lost track. The best she could figure it might have been a week. Enough time passed that Elizabeth no longer believed that Pete would return. Hope had receded, diminished and disappeared with each hour, with each sunrise. There was none left. Rationally and emotionally, she came to know he wouldn't return; that he couldn't.

In a pine log cabin, across Little Mountain, across Devil's Canyon a short distance south from Duggar Flat and Hannon's Cooley, she knew. Now it

46

was just her and her alone with Pike the dog. No one could survive that kind of cold with a rifle, a sheepskin coat and a pair of mittens. No one. Not for that long Not Pete nor anyone else. *Probably not me, either.*

As this realization came she knew that no one would come. She couldn't stay and live. She couldn't and wouldn't live if she stayed. She knew.

Instead of waiting for her husband she waited for the storm to lift. If she was to have any chance she'd have to leave the cabin early. She'd have to walk out of the canyon and across Little Mountain. Except Little Mountain wasn't little and Low Mountain certainly wasn't low. It was miles and miles of miles and miles of flat grass land. She could only take with her what she could carry.

During the lonely days and nights she planned. She'd wear her pants, and Pete's pants over that; she'd wear her shirts and Pete's shirts over hers; she'd wear his only pair of silk stocks, then her socks, then Pete's other socks and last Pete's boots; she'd wear her mittens under Pete's mittens with a scarf around her head; she'd fix it so she could breathe and see out, but barely. That is what she'd wear when the weather broke; if it broke. She knew she'd have to be ready if it did, when it did. There would be no second chances. No do-overs. She'd have one chance and it would be her only chance.

She glanced at Pike. "You and me, dog. You and me."

The weather broke on the thirteenth day following Pete's failure to return. Down below, off the mountain, on the Big Horn River, the temperature had dropped to forty below. Between the river and the Canyon walls the ice was thick, the snow deep. On Little Mountain it was colder. It was early morning when she started off the mountain. For breakfast she ate potatoes and pancakes like it was her last meal, like she'd never eat again. What she didn't eat she stuck in her pockets and her husband's pant pockets. The latter she filled with a handful of jerky. There was no use in taking water. It would freeze within minutes of stepping outside.

It was time.

She opened the door and left it open. Pike immediately ran outside, looking back at her as if he to ask "which way?" She started walking, trying to maneuver around snowdrifts taller than herself. It was three steps forward and two steps back and so bright that she could barely see though squinted eyes. Pike stayed out front, occasionally looking back at her struggling in the snow.

She made it into Devil's Canyon, across Porcupine Creek and up the other side. Somewhere on top of Little Mountain she lost the feeling in her feet. Perhaps it was the snow in her boots or the snow in her pants. Somewhere she lost feeling in her fingers, then on her ears, her cheeks and chin. Somewhere on the Mountain the baby stopped kicking. For its sake she tried to hurry. But there was no hurry; there was simply one step in front of another.

When she fell she got up. The bright sunlight bounced off the snow, limiting her sight to glaring white, burning her eyes until she could no longer see. To compensate, she tied a small rope, a strap, around Pike's neck. He led. He pulled. She followed.

Somewhere she lost her sense of direction and simply went with the wind. Fortunately, it was blowing off the mountain, south and west, toward the river. Fortunately, Pike seemed to know where she wanted to go and kept moving.

Elizabeth walked, fell, walked and walked and kept walking. It was her chance; her only chance. It was the baby's only chance. When she was thirsty, she put snow in her mouth then wrapped the scarf tightly around her head, holding her ears against her head. They stung, they ached. As she walked, the scarf grew loose until she no longer cared. And she walked. Her world was white because snow is white. Somehow, by some miracle she navigated to the southern escarpments of Little Mountain one step at a time. She followed the damn dog and somehow climbed off the mountain until the relentless wind no longer pursued her and she simply stopped, unable to take another step.

Dan Beal, a young man of eighteen, sitting on a grey saddle horse, found her standing in a pool of water and ice several yards from the frozen expanse of the Big Horn River. It was mid-day. But for the barking of a dog he would have missed her. Pike was barking and Dan looked to see why. The dog wanted her to keep moving. She didn't. She couldn't. When Dan tried to get close, the dog barred the way. Finally, he got her on his horse and took her across the river. Carl Fink's cabin was the closest. Dan took her there.

In her delirium Elizabeth didn't know that she'd been found. The dog was making a racket, barking continuously; then there was someone. She heard a voice. She felt hands that lifted and carried. Warm blankets: relief from the cold, the endless wind. Soft, anxious voices.

"Poor dear," the voices said.

"What happened?" the voices asked. Above her were shadows of people she couldn't see, didn't know.

"Put her feet in a pan of cold water."

"What? She is freezing. She's froze. She don't need no ice water!"

"Do what I'm tellin' you. Put her feet in ice water. Every five minutes pour a cup of hot water in the pan. Rub her feet in between. Do it. Keep doin' it 'til the water in the pan is warm and I tell you to stop."

"Who told you that?"

"Mother."

"I ain't heard that before."

"Would you just do it? And get a sock cap for her head. It'll press her ears against her head. But not too tight. Hear me? Not too tight."

"What?"

"Just do it."

"Your mother?"

"Just do it."

"I'm just doin' it."

"Get one of the kids in here. No, two. Have them each take a hand and rub it. Start at the forearm. Rub to the fingers. Over and over."

"Honey..."

"I ain't got time to explain. I gotta build up the fire. Gotta heat up some more water. Boy, fetch the mule. Go get ol' Doc Neeley. Be quick about it."

"I was gonna say we'll be needin' more hot water."

"Sorry. I don't mean nothing..."

"It's all right. I knows what you're doin'"

"I'm sure as hell glad someone does. Shut the door, would you, boy?"

A door closed. Soft voices washed over her.

"Who is she?"

"Looks like Pete's woman."

"Where'd she come from?"

"Little Mountain."

"In this weather? How'd she do that?"

"God knows. I sure as hell don't."

"Wonder where Pete is." Silence. "I suppose you're gonna tell me God knows."

"Right now He's the only one."

Later there was another man's voice and other women. Someone touched her cheeks with hot fingers. Her hands began to tingle and ache. Someone told her to sleep. Someone put a hot towel on her forehead. Someone forced her to drink hot soup. Someone wrapped her in blankets. Someone saved her life.

Somehow, somewhere she slept, wondering if she was dream walking, wondering if Pete was going to walk through the door cursing the cold, looking at the stove for something to eat. She drifted off to sleep wondering if her baby was going to start kicking again.

Epilogue

Elizabeth Gervay survived, suffering from severe frostbite, losing some toes, some fingers, parts of her ears. Her baby did not. Not long after she was discovered standing in the ice water, yards from the Big Horn River, a party of men backtracked her as far as they could. Her husband's body was located along a game trail in Devil's Canyon. Apparently, he suffered a fall and a broken leg. He had gotten a deer but was unable to get back to Elizabeth because of his injuries and the cold. He and his baby were buried together in a square casket in the Iona Cemetery. A square casket was necessary because his body was frozen and rigor mortis had set in, making it a requirement. Since then, time destroyed the marker and it is impossible to tell exactly where in the cemetery he and the child lay. May they rest in peace.

Elizabeth Gervay regained her health and in the late spring simply disappeared. No one knows where she went. Maybe back to Chicago. She was from there, or so someone said. No one knows. Another someone said she got on the train in Kane but didn't know which direction she chose. The west, big, brawley and unforgiving, simply took her in. She was never heard from again.

Pike, the dog, hung around Carl Fink's house waiting for Elizabeth to recover. After she left, he followed the trail herds north into the Dryhead country. He disappeared, too. A coyote probably got him. That was the rumor.

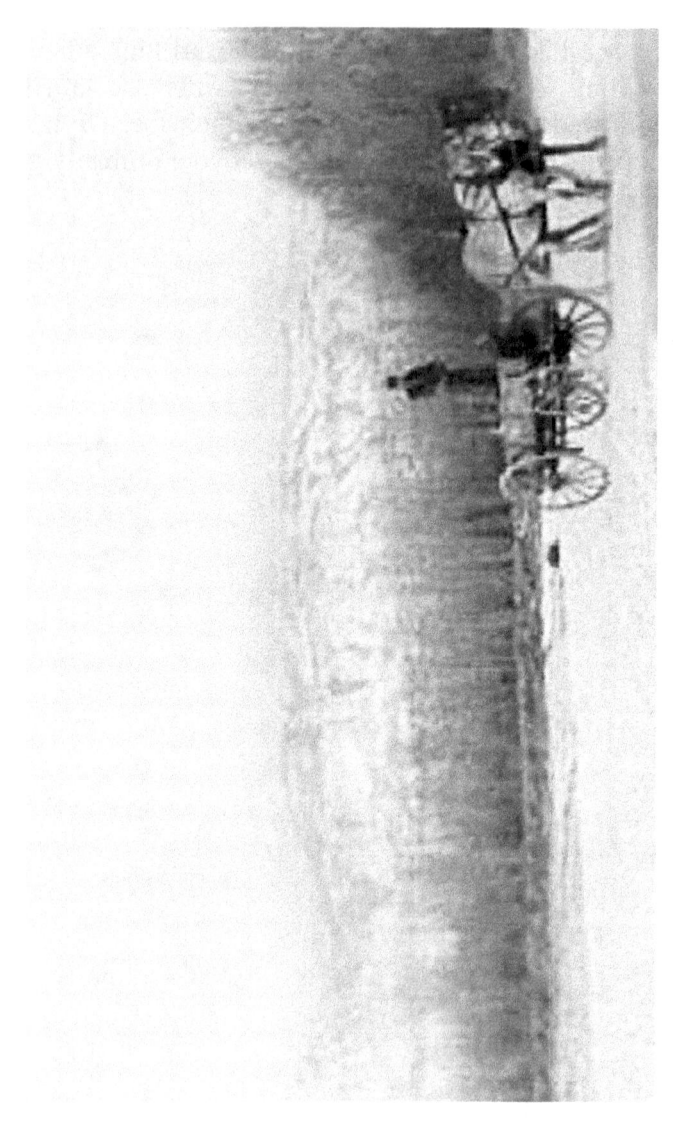

Low Mountain in Winter

Martha Pearl and Newel "Red" Howe

CHAPTER 6

BOY WITH A LANTERN

The moon hung low over Sheep Mountain, casting shadows long and dim across the wide expanse of river. In the moonlit darkness the Horn's currents ran silent and deep, swirling amid the rustle of cottonwood leaves, the aching croak of frogs, and the sharp piercing cry of swallows. A breeze drifted down the canyon and out into the valley, bringing the smell of sage brush and grass drying on the stem. With it lingered the portent of fall. A coyote sang, its voice rising, then vanishing. On the west side of the river, running past the limestone caves, the rails of the Chicago, Burlington & Quincy hummed of a train coming. It was miles away and would pass through Himes as if Himes wasn't there. It wasn't there; not really, for Himes was just a name signifying some dirt, rocks, clumps of greasewood and sagebrush. Himes was a thought that had never materialized, a dream unrealized and unfulfilled.

On the east side of the river at the northern mouth the canyon was a stand of cottonwood trees, the oldest of which was alive when Washington crossed the icy Delaware. A dull lamplight reflected against the leaves of those trees and extended a short distance down a dirt road on one side and out into the river on the other. If a man had been standing on Old Bald Mountain high on the

Big Horns, ten thousand feet above sea level, he would have been able to see it, a small candle gleaming in the hundreds of thousands of acres that was the Big Horn Basin. From up there he could have seen it all. But there would be no man watching.

Half an hour later when the freight train passed Sheep Mountain Canyon the engineer would not see it. It would be gone.. Now there was only the flickering glimmer of a kerosene lantern in a grove of cottonwood trees.

"Hold that lantern steady would you, Boy?"

"Yes, sir," the boy replied looking down from the tree limb at the man.

"How you doin' up there? You gonna make it?"

"Yes, sir," the red headed lad said, nodding his head. He sat perched in the crook of a cottonwood, his feet braced against a dead limb, the lantern's handle firmly in his fingers. The bottom of the lantern sat on the dead branch. His grip steadied it, keeping it from falling to the earth below. The dead branch took all of its weight and that of the boy. The lad was steadfast in his chore as he watched his uncles butchering a yearling steer. A summer breeze played with his hair, tickling his forehead as he watched.

The tall man glanced toward the two room shack.

"Martha, keep an eye on that boy, would you? Don't want him fallin' out of that tree and breakin' a leg."

"I am, Lou. Why'd you put him up there anyways? He's so small."

The tall, angular man removed his hat and scratched his head before reseating it. He looked at the boy sitting on the tree limb before answering.

"Hard to get in trouble sittin' in a tree. We're 'bout done. Got a pan? I'll fetch you the heart and liver."

The short statured woman disappeared inside the shack, her long skirts rustling. He could hear women's voices. Someone inside laughed. He glanced again at the boy in the tree and wondered what was funny. His brother had attached the hind legs of the carcass to the single-tree. They were ready to pull the yearling up and hang it from a tree branch. Lou thought about using his saddle horse. No use pulling the steer up by hand. Not if they could help it.

"Jess," he said, "keep an eye on the boy. I'll get the saddle horse. We'll hoist the carcass up. Looks like we're close to being done."

"All right" was the quiet reply.

Once they had the carcass hanging, Lou started the skinning, cutting the hide, peeling it away from the muscle. Jess helped, then busied himself slitting the belly from brisket to tail, dropping the entrails onto the hide, careful not to nick an intestine and spoil the meat. He separated the heart and liver, putting them into the pan that Martha had handed him.

The moon dropped behind Sheep Mountain leaving them in its shadow. Except for the night

58

birds and the river, there were no sounds. The boy coughed.

Both men looked up at him.

"Sis, better get that boy outta' that tree. I keep worryin' he'll fall, land on his head an' break that lantern."

"Really, Lou. The lantern? You're concerned about the lantern?"

"Sure wouldn't hurt that boy's head."

"All right," she replied, looking at Lou, then the tree. "In case you two hadn't noticed I'm not quite that tall. I will need some help."

"Get a ladder, Sis."

She turned to look at the two men.

"Just teasing," Lou laughed. "I'll get the boy."

Lantern and boy were lifted from the dead cottonwood limb. Red stood among what to him were tall people and watched as his Uncle began to pile the center of the hide spread out on the ground with rock.

His uncle glanced at him. "Gonna help, boy, or did someone nail your shoes to the ground?"

"Why are you pilin' it with rocks?"

"Ballast. Need to weigh it down so it don't swim away."

"Why?"

"Seems like the thing to do."

"Oh"

"You gonna help or just stand there?"

Red started gathering rocks to supplement those his uncle had collected. The lantern was taken inside. In the near-darkness, Jess finished butchering the steer, trimming away fat, saving it for the dog. The boy followed Lou as he hefted the hide filled with rock and entrails, carrying it to the river bank. Swinging it, once, twice, releasing it, tossing it as far as he could, they watched it splash and sink into dark waters.

Lou stared up at the expansive sky. A cloud, its underside still lit by the sinking moon, hung high over Sheep Mountain. Somewhere there was a thunderstorm. He could hear it rattling far way.

Maybe as far as the Absorkas. Probably not that far. Probably somewhere near West Pryor. Near Warren or Frannie maybe.

Once the moon had dropped behind Sheep Mountain, stars began to appear. The boy stood quietly beside his uncle, waiting. Both watched the river, listening.

"See that, Boy? See those stars above the Pryor?" He pointed. "If you look, you'll see the outline of a dipper. There's the handle. There's the outline of a cup. See it?"

"I do."

"Look at the side of the dipper. The cup. See those two stars. If you look, you'll see they point at another. That one out there way above the East Pryor all alone, by itself. See it? That's the North Star, Boy. That's the one you'll want to remember. It never moves. It's always there. Remember that, boy. Remember it and you'll never be lost."

"Why?"

"Well, Boy, I'll tell you. If you are somewheres and you don't know upside down from Sunday, wait 'til dark, look at the heavens, locate the Big Dipper, then find that star--that one right there hanging in the sky. That star will tell you which way is north. It never changes. It is always there. If you know where north is then you'll know which way is south and east and west. You'll be able to find your way home. You'll never be lost for long. Ok, Boy?"

"Ok."

The tall man glanced at the boy staring into the heavens.

"You hungry, Red? What do you say we go inside and slobber all over fresh cut steak? See if that steer is worth eatin'?"

"Shouldn't we cook it?"

Lou laughed. He paused and looked fondly at the small boy."I suppose maybe we should," he said. "Run it by the stove a couple of times." He paused again, mussing his hair. "What? Don't you like raw meat?"

"I don't think I do."

"But you like stars?"

The boy glanced up toward the Pryors and the North star.

"That one is pretty," he said. "It just stays there."

"You're right about that, Boy. It just stays there."

Red continued. "And if we look we can always find the mountain 'cause that mountain and that star is always there." Red paused thinking. "Uncle Lou, where is it in the day time?"

"It's there, Red. Even in the daytime. In the daylight we just can't see it. But it is there."

"Oh."

They stood there for another moment. A fish jumped, its splash breaking the silence. The frogs started their croaking sound.

From the canyon they heard the whistle of the freight train as it came barreling down the tracks. One long. Two short.

"Uncle Lou? I think the train is coming."

"I think you're right, Boy."

It was the summer of 1916. In a few months Louis Howe and Forest Eugene Howe would be in France packing aught-sixes, fixing bayonets, dodging bullets, and avoiding poison gas. But on this night, Red's child support had been unilaterally collected and received with gratitude and the North Star was where it was supposed to be. No one begged the county attorney for help with a derelict dad. No one said a word. No one complained. No one cast aspersions. Instead, the family sat at a pinewood table, ate fresh steak cooked medium rare, salted to taste. Someone mentioned that the grass was good that summer, that it had rained more this year than last, and that Rose was going to Kane this coming Friday for some ribbon and to get her shoe fixed. Maybe she should pick up some sugar if it wasn't too much trouble. In two weeks Jess was going to start weaning the spring calves. That would be a noisy ruckus. Nobody was going to be able to sleep once that started. Nice though to get it done.

In a corner of the next room, buried under blankets and pillows, a small boy slept. He dreamed of skipping rocks across the flat surface of the river, of the "damn" dog, Ring chasing rabbits and spring calves when he shouldn't. When he was supposed to, he would be off running around, nowhere to be found. And there above the East Pryor Mountain was the North Star, where it was supposed to be, where it had always been.

Irish Parks and Newel Howe and Kane School
Wagon

CHAPTER 7

STUDENT OUT OF CLASS

Jess Howe rode down from the high Pryor country after the first snow fell and stayed, cold and white above the timberline. He sat easily in the saddle, more a part of it than not. The sun had burned him brown except where his hat rested low on his forehead. There the skin was unnaturally white. The light brown hair that tumbled over his collar was long, but not so long as to call undue attention to it.

Fall had been a little cold at seven thousand feet elevation, so he wore a sheepskin coat loosely around his shoulders. It hung to mid-thigh covering his holstered pistol, a leather strap securing the hammer and revolver. He never used it much. It was for rabbits, rattlesnakes and to make sure his brother Lou didn't lose fist fights. Who knew when you'd need something like that? There was no telling, so he kept it handy.

He rode into Kane from the north side, turning neither left nor right, staying pretty much to the center of the dusty gravel road. It was close to two-fifteen in the afternoon. Except for the horse he was riding, he looked like any other horseman passing through on a balmy Thursday. This horse, however, was a little better than most, stood a little taller, moved with a certain grace that was unmistakable.

On his left was a log school house with a cedar rail hitching post on two sides and a buggy belonging to the school teacher out back. The building itself was set back from the road under a cottonwood tree just above the canal. A mile down the dirt and gravel road he could see the top of the Neely hotel and that of the First State Bank. Both of these buildings were across the street from the Kane Post Office and the General Store built out of gyp block. The section house stood by the railroad across the street from the hog pens and pool hall.

All of these matters of city planning were seen by the horseman as he rode toward the settlement. Come evening he'd be fording the river at Himes at the mouth of Sheep Canyon. He'd be home, such as it was.

In front of the school younger children were playing "kick the can". Out in front on the road three of the older boys were sitting on the rail fence that separated street from school and roadway and kept the school fenced in. They were arguing, bantering back and forth, as the horseman approached. No one remembered the man. He hadn't been seen before, so they jawed back and forth about who he was, who he wasn't, and who he might be. One claimed to have seen the horse, but it was agreed that no one knew the rider. Then no one knew the horse, either.

One ventured that it could be "that Jess fellow" folks talked about, that no one had seen, except maybe Fred the hostler and John Smith the

Ferryman. But they all agreed that that fellow was dead for sure; that he'd been shot and crawled off somewhere, hid himself, and died a lonely death in some hole. After all, that's what those two drunks had said when they got all liquored up at Harvey's Saloon, Bar and Grill, uptown Lovell.

The "kick the can" gang swirled around them, under the fence, to the edge of the roadway and back under the fence. Left in its wake was a red-headed six year old who also saw the horse, the rider. Only he didn't step back. He stepped forward. One step, two, three, then he was out in the middle of the road.

The boy on the end yelled a warning. All three jumped down and tried to reach him, but they were too late the heroes. A hand reached down from the blue October sky and pulled the lad up, placing him deftly on the shoulders of the saddle. The boy, Red, leaned back, wrapping the sheep skin around himself until only his red head and brown eyes showed. The long sorrel horse never missed a step; never stopped, never hesitated, never slowed down.

The boy snuggled against the rider, and looked up at his whiskered chin. "Where have you been, Uncle Jess?" he asked. "I've been waiting really, really long. And I don't like school much."

"Cowboyin'. Lookin' for strays," he said, his voice a rumble deep in his chest.

"Did you get any?"

"The only stray I got is you, kid. I got you."

Red smiled happily. "I'm glad you did, Uncle Jess. Uncle Lou, Uncle Far and mom, we was worryin', you bein' gone so long and it gettin' cold."

Jess glanced down at the boy's head. He asked, "Just how "gone so long" was I Red? Five days ain't all that much."

"Pretty long, Uncle Jess. Me waitin' and having to go to school and all. Pretty dang long I suspect."

It was the rider's turn to smile.

First Kane School and the "Kick the can" gang. "Red" is in the first row, second from the left

Inside the Classroom of Kane's Brick Schoolhouse

CHAPTER 8

WOMAN ON THE EDGE

The raven was coal black, old and worn. Its feathers were ruffled about its neck as if it had been in a long fight, and had not fared well. The skinny woman from the porch watched it light on the cottonwood limb in front of the two story house. A flock of barn sparrows immediately began darting at it, diving quickly, flipping to the right and left at the very last minute. Several struck at its head, causing it to duck under the winged assault. A few minutes passed. The raven grew tired of the aerial bombardment and took flight with a red-wing blackbird and a sparrow dutifully chasing it, making sure.

The woman watched, thinking about the raven, its black, flashing, eyes.

Twenty-eight minutes later the raven returned, perching on a corral gate post, hopping to a pole then lofting itself and gliding to the apex of the barn's roof. Momentarily it disappeared, landing on the other side of the roof before it waddled back into view, perching on the worn shingles above the hay loft and double doorway. It waited, cocking its head to one side, then the other, watching, its black eyes blinking.

A gust of wind blew up, dust swirling, ruffling its already ruffled feathers. In the flurry it took flight, catching the breeze on stiff wings, drifting toward the cottonwood timber on the Shoshone river bottom three quarters of a mile away. It again was chased--this time by a single sparrow.

It was the fifth time the woman had watched the raven.

It'll be back, she thought. *It always comes back.* She stared after the retreating figure until the raven became a tiny dark speck that disappeared altogether.

Matilda was a stick woman, thin and gaunt, her eyes retreating slightly into her head, and a wisp of dark brown hair dangling across her forehead. For days, months and years she had dutifully waited for her man to come home from chasing cows, fixing fences, digging ditches, or irrigating the graze in the west pasture. In the afternoon and late evening the man, bowlegged and tired, would return, riding a dun horse, smelling of horse sweat and branding smoke, with blood on his shirt and levis from dehorning and castrating bull calves; lice lived in his unwashed and matted hair. He'd need a bath but it wasn't Saturday. Not yet. That was three days away. The stick woman was thirty-seven years old living in a fifty-four year old frame house painted white. The house sat under a canopy of cottonwood up against a hill that rose behind it, protecting it from the north winds that blew in winter.

The raven hadn't returned.

This Thursday her man returned from the pastures on the north mountain; he'd been gone ten days. Through the front window she watched him dismount, swing the corral gate open and lead the dun inside, pulling the saddle, letting it fall to the ground, then removing the bridle. A few minutes later, he sat slouched on the threadbare coach, tired and worn out. In minutes he was asleep. He hadn't said a word to her; not that she expected it.

Outside, her smallest boy was playing in the dirt under the elm tree: playing with a block of wood, imagining it was a buckboard, rolling it on imaginary roads, up imaginary hills and into imaginary barns. A few minutes passed; he was shrieking at his older brother, trying in vain to drive him away. The woman thought of going out on the porch to stop the conflict but she didn't. Once the shrieks failed, invariably, the youngest would be throwing rocks and sticks, and anything else at hand. That's the way it was for the youngest was four, the other five, and neither could leave the other alone.

Her man was asleep, still sitting upright, too tired to eat, too tired to go to bed. Outside, the brotherly conflict hadn't fully risen yet; she wondered how much longer her husband's slumber would last, or if it would. She'd stare at his shirt, the torn pocket, thinking about cleaning it, mending it. It was no use. Blood had stained it permanently, adding to the stack of stained shirts, of torn levis, of shirts in need of repair, of socks whose heels needing darning. To escape the thought, she walked out onto the porch to listen to the boys argue.

Once outside she glanced back through the open doorway into the kitchen, past her sleeping man, the worn sofa, the stained shirt with the torn pocket, the half full sack of Bull Durham. A half pail of water rested on the black cookstove but there was no fire to heat the water. Wood. She needed wood from the woodpile. None was chopped; the axe blade dull. Dishes had piled up on the counter; none clean, all dirty with grease, gravy, and crusts of bread, dried egg yolk and grits. At the end of the counter the bread dough had risen in the pan until it seemed about to pour over the sides. It needed to be punched down before it rolled onto the counter and fell onto the floor and she was forced to throw it out to the chickens.

She shook her head, thinking about the raven, remembering the baby needed changing, to be dressed, as well as fed. Her blouse, wet from her breasts leaking milk, reminded her the infant was still asleep in her crib. In spite of her discomfort she refused to wake her. It occurred to her that she hadn't eaten herself. She mused, hoping the baby would wake up soon. She wanted to sit down, wondering what she could eat. In all of the kitchen what was there to eat? It had been so long. Oh, she thought, I am so tired; my arms and legs so heavy, like lead weights. I can hardly lift them.

Her husband stirred on the sofa. The older boy was poking the younger's shoulder with a stick. The younger had grabbed the stick in both hands.

She sat down on the porch chair mindful of the baby's sighs, her leaking breasts, her wet blouse. The raven had returned. *So soon*, she thought, seeing him perched once again on the apex of the barn's roof. *What did that bird want?* He had returned, only to be harassed by sparrows and blackbirds. *Why?*

In two hours Walt Beeden would be riding up the lane from the county road. He'd be sitting on the school bus seat above the jockey box talking to the single mare that pulled the bus. He'd say, "Afternoon, Mrs. Waters." Sometimes he'd say nothing at all as he watched the three kids get off of the bus. Mostly he said, "Afternoon, Mrs. Waters." That's what he said. Nothing more.

Looking up, she was surprised for there he was.This day he said nothing to her.

Inside the bus were her two older sons, and her daughter. They got off last because they got on first. The boys stepped down from the horse drawn bus first. The older shoved his younger brother, taunting him.

"Out of the way, runt," he said.

Her daughter saw her standing on the veranda. "Hi mom," she greeted her gaily, then she ran inside and upstairs, walking past the baby sitting unchanged in her crib, over a pile of dirt on the floor, the rising bread floating out of the breadpan, the dirty dishes, the cold water sitting in the bucket on the cold stove.

What did she expect? Ruth May was eight, only eight. Her room needed cleaning; her clothes needed washing; her stuff needed to be picked up from the floor, from the chest of drawers, from the chair in the corner, from the bed.

Her thoughts dwelled on washing clothes but there was no hot water. None. Her thoughts wandered to the water barrel. *Was there any left?* Saturday she'd washed clothes, the dishes, and she'd scrubbed the counters, the table. How much had she used? It was only a fifty-five gallon barrel. There'd be less because her man hadn't filled it to the top. All the way from the river more had slopped out. *Little was left*, she thought. *Not much.* Her man would either get some more or there'd be no bath, no clean clothes, nothing to cook with. Nothing to eat. He'd be upset; he'd go to the river in the wagon.

She stood and stared at the barn and the dun horse standing in the corral, its head down. Worrying her hands, she searched the cottonwood limbs in front of the house, the roof of the barn, the gatepost, looking for the raven.

To her surprise it flew out of the barn through the double doors and lit on the gatepost that held the sagging gate. In its beak it had something, something that moved. It was a struggling bird, a baby bird. Following the raven from the barn were three sparrows. They flung themselves at the much larger raven, cutting and diving. The raven didn't seem to mind. It took flight with the smaller birds darting after it, chasing it toward the river bottom with the small, struggling infant, barely out of the egg, seized tightly in its bill.

Standing in the doorway, the stick woman held herself very still for several minutes. She tried to get her thoughts around what she'd just witnessed, her mind settling on the doomed baby barn sparrow, which even now was being torn asunder, supper for a raven, for the raven's brood. She imagined six featherless birds sitting in a larger nest, their billed mouths open wide begging for life giving meat; the baby sparrow. *My God, she thought. My God in heaven.*

Matilda Waters woke with a start. The house was dead quiet. Her husband gone. What day was it? Not day. No. It was night. It was dark. Her husband was not there. Where was he? Disoriented, she got up from the sofa and stepped outside onto the veranda.

Across the yard sitting on the corral gate post was the raven. It had a bird in its beak. Not a baby, but a sparrow. Another, perhaps the raven's mate, was perched on the gate itself. It, too, had a bird grasped firmly in its beak. Even in the dark, she could see the captured bird moving, its eyes blinking, its legs jerking, quivering as it faced death.

Soon, very soon, somewhere down on the river, the captured bird would be pulled apart; perhaps alive; pieces dropped into open mouths; filling squawking, gaping beaks, all open wide, demanding meat, demanding more and more and more.

The ravens. Oh my God, they've come for me. They've come for John Robert, for Ruth, for Junior. They've come for the baby. The baby? Not the baby. The baby was dead. No, not her. No. No. The baby wasn't dead. Where was the baby? She didn't remember. *Mary? Mary? Mary? Where are you, Mary?*

The raven had flown, but even in flight he was looking at her. She saw it clearly: the black round eye staring; its mouth trapped the struggling sparrow.

It'd be back. They always came back. Oh my God. There is nothing I can do. Nothing at all. There's no water in the bucket. No wood. There's no wood. She wanted to scream. She opened her mouth. Nothing came out.

The house was dark. She hurried inside. There was no time. *The ravens. The ravens would be back. They always come back. Only this time there are no sparrows.*

Hurriedly, she retrieved the .22 rifle from the closet. Automatically, she checked the magazine. It was loaded. Fully loaded. *There's no time. No time at all.*

Outside she heard the ravens, their ugly squawking, the sparrow in its mouth. Down on the river in the nest of ravens the mouths were open wide.

She fled upstairs. The dark ravens were coming. She had to hurry.

Quietly, she opened Ruth May's door, not wanting to wake the slumbering child. But it was dark. She couldn't see. She switched the light on. The forty watt bulb glowed softly lighting the room in dull yellow. In her bed the child was asleep in her blankets, one leg sticking out.

Matilda put the barrel of the .22 behind the sleeping child's ear and pulled the trigger. In the room the report was incredibly loud. The child didn't move. Matilda quietly switched the light off, not wanting to wake her, and closed the door. She went to the next room and the next and the next. Quickly, she went to the last bedroom, hers. This time she glanced out the window.

Just as Matilda thought, downstairs the raven was sitting on the veranda's railing, walking back and forth, waiting, cocking its head one way then the other. But this raven waited in vain for she had finished her tasks. There was no water. There was no wood. The axe was dull and the shirts needed mending.

Mary? Mary? Baby, where are you? It's time to eat. I really need to feed you. I can't wait any longer.

Putting the barrel of the .22 rifle in her mouth, she pulled the trigger. The ravens weren't going to get her. Her body collapsed to the bedroom floor, sprawled across the .22 rifle.

Below the house, halfway to the river, the tracks of the Chicago, Burlington and Quincy had started to hum. Upline, the freight train, pulling twenty-eight cars, and a caboose had just left the outskirts of the town of Lovell, bound for Greybull and the train yards under the hill. There a new train would be made up and cattle cars sent through Worland, Thermopolis, Shoshone and, finally, Fort Casper. Next week would find the cars in Chicago, unloading Hereford steers in the largest stockyards ever built. Before the cattle cars had passed through Omaha, Nebraska and Des Moines, Iowa, Matilda Waters would be buried next to her four children on

79

the rocky knoll two miles north of the Church in Iona.

Footnote: On the evening of May 11, 1921 Matilda Waters, wife of James Waters, mother of John Robert, Junior Dee, Ruth May, Paul Herbert, and the baby, Mary, went from bedroom to bedroom and shot four of her children, killing them. Then, turning the weapon on herself, killed herself. The baby Mary had died the year before on May 5, 1920. Matilda was buried in the Iona Cemetery, Big Horn County, State of Wyoming. Her body rests by the gate along the north fence. Her solitary tombstone reads, "Matilda 1884-1921" She was buried on that rocky knoll ninety-one years ago last month. Nothing marks her passing except a stone, some greasewood, a twig of sagebrush, and some solitary bunch grass. She was born on August 7, 1884 and was 37 years old when she shot herself. If you want to ask "why?" don't. No one knows the answer.

Matilda Water's Headstone, Iona Cemetery

80

CHAPTER 9

MONUMENT TO RILEY KANE

In 1896 an event of some note occurred in the Big Horn Basin, Territory of Wyoming.

Bill Cody took up residence at the west end of the Basin and thereafter built the Irma Hotel, Grill, Bar and Eatery. Some say Cody, Wyoming was born the summer of that year. Bill Cody thought so.

Ten years later in 1906 at the north east end of the Basin on the Big Horn River, the Chicago, Quincy and Burlington Railroad built corrals to service the great ML Ranch and its twenty-five thousand head of cattle. These corrals were built east of the tracks. On the other side of those tracks lay the town limits of Kane, Wyoming.

Kane was established before 1906 as a direct result of the activities of Tony Mason and Hank Lovell. The date of this event is difficult to establish accurately. In 1879 Lovell and Mason brought 12,500 head of cattle into the basin. In the succeeding years they built their ranch buildings on the east side of the Big Horn River three plus miles south of its confluence with the Shoshone. This construction took a few years.

In 1880, Mason and Lovell brought another 12,500 head from Oregon into the basin. Twenty-five thousand head of cattle required a goodly number of hands to care for them. To give the years of 1879

81

and 1880 some historical reference, it was in 1876 one hundred miles north that George Armstrong Custer met Crazy Horse on the Greasy Grass. That's a mere thirty six months.

Kane, Wyoming was probably born sometime after these two events. It had an inauspicious beginning. A man named Riley Kane built a log cabin on the west side of the Big Horn River and started a general store to service the commercial needs of the cowhands that worked for the ML ranch. Later, he was also the foreman for the ML Ranch. So the town of Kane commenced after 1880, for certain. It commenced as a commercial entity when Riley Kane built his log cabin/store. The exact date is not known. It more likely than not was in 1881 or 1882.

Certainly Kane's store was constructed prior to 1890 and probably at the approximate time the ML cowhands brought cattle to the area and needed to purchase supplies. Eventually Riley moved to Shell, Wyoming where he died and is buried. It should be noted that the ML also had additional ranch buildings in Shell.

Some say that Riley Kane thought it disingenuous to have a town named after him. On the other hand Bill Cody thought he deserved to have a town named after him, since he was famous for shooting buffalo and an Indian named Yellow Hand, without himself being killed. It helped that he was a showman with a need for publicity.

In the name of civic progress, Riley Kane's boss, Henry Clay Lovell was named Kane's first postmaster. He was hardly ever there. If mail got misdirected it sure as hell wasn't his fault. No matter: Hank also had a town named after him. Lovell, Wyoming is situated twelve miles west of Kane on the Shoshone river. It bears Henry's surname today.

The fact is, that Kane, that sore or diamond on the body politic of the Big Horn Basin, was forever named after a cowhand, the ramrod for Tony Mason and Hank Lovell. Bill Cody was a showman. He knew people. Riley Kane knew cows. That's why the ML had so many. And that's the way he wanted to keep it. As a note of passing interest: Bill Cody didn't give a damn about cows. And that is how he wanted to keep it.

After the construction of the log building that housed Kane and his store the settlement grew. It eventually added the State Bank, a hotel, another store, a pool hall, a library/community center, a brick school house, a gold mine, a number of houses and a hog pen.

The Chicago, Quincy and Burlington section house became a two story affair painted a deep railroad red with white lettering. A platform was built out of brick to service the freight and passenger trains. It stretched a good fifty yards along a double set of tracks and covered the cistern that serviced the steam engines and the section house. Everyone used it for drinking water. No one seemed to mind that the water belonged to the railroad. It had two green iron wheeled carts for hauling luggage from the baggage car. They assisted folks getting off the train carrying more than a sandwich, two carrots and an apple.

CHAPTER 10

WOMAN AT THE DEPOT

Rosanna Porter had a Tuesday practice of going to the Chicago, Burlington and Quincy train depot in Kane, Wyoming, sitting on the green wooden bench half way down the platform, and watching the 3:44 passenger train roll in, coming to a stop in a marvelous burst of steam and sound. If she had an apple she'd nibble on it, taking small bites so that it would last. Presumably, the train would arrive on time. Often it would not. It was of no matter to her. She'd still wait to see who got off and who got on. She was sixty-four years old and had plenty to do, but on Tuesday she didn't want to do any of those things.

Some folks say she'd seen a lot. She'd been a twig of a girl when her father put their wagon into the Wind River miles south of Thermopolis. Her brothers were out front wading. They'd bob up and down laughing and yelling when they hit a deep hole and the water was over their heads. Having been warned, her dad would try and miss the deep water, intent on saving the wagon and everything they owned. That's how she came into the Basin with her brothers wading in the river and walking down the middle of Wind River Canyon. Rosanna sat on the wagon seat with her father and mother, his hands full of the ribbons, his eyes on the team of blacks pulling the wagon, sometimes swimming, sometimes pulling when their hooves found purchase on the rocky river bottom.

That was the only time she remembered her mother not reprimanding her brothers for getting their shoes wet. She was ten. Her brothers were twelve and fourteen.

"Why Rosanna, whatever are you doing sitting here?"

Rosanna looked up, the sun at her back casting the long rays of afternoon from over the grey hills behind and the pointed hill, euphemistically called Katy's Nipple. *Truthfully that name*!

As an eleven year old, and nearly every year thereafter, she had climbed those very heights and scratched her name in the sandstone rocks at the top with a nail the blacksmith made. Her name was still there. She looked. At the very top you could see everywhere (the river bottom anyway): south almost to Himes and the Kane Caves and north to the Narrows at the foot of Low Mountain where that strange man Frank Sykes lived. Up there on the Nipple the wind never stopped blowing. And like every other girl who lived in Kane, Wyoming she wondered who Katie was, what she did, and how she came to get her name and bodily appendage attached to that hill.

"I could say the same to you, Garvin. Come sit down." Rosanna scooted over, making some room. "I've come to watch the train. I like to see people getting on and getting off."

"I'm here to fill my water cans," he said.

86

"Yes, I know. Every Tuesday."

"You do? I mean you're here every Tuesday, yourself?"

"Not when it rains or if it's cold. I don't like sitting here when it's cold," Rosanna replied

The bench creaked as it accepted his weight.

"I must be blind."

"You are. You pump your cans full, load them in the back of your wagon, then you go to the post office. Afterwards you go to the store."

"Well, I'll be damned."

"You will be you keep talking like that."

Garvin Porter laughed. "You've been watching, girl."

"Since Melvin died, once a week I come here. Gets me out of the house...."

"That's five years."

"Almost," she said. "Five years in two months. But who's counting? Certainly not me."

"You walk all that way every Tuesday? he asked."

"It's not but a mile, Garvin. I'm a widow woman. I ain't dead."

"That's for damn sure."

"Garvin, must you? she asked."

""Must I what?"

"Curse."

"I sure as hell hope not."

Rosanna laughed.

"I miss him," he said absently.

"One does miss one's brother once he's dead."

Garvin smiled and glanced at her. "I guess one does," he drawled.

"You making fun of the way I talk?"

"I love the way you talk."

"Why don't you come listen to me talk more often?"

Garvin smiled, looking at Rosanna. She was staring down the tracks. "I should," he said. He paused, reflecting. "You don't know how close I come to marryin' you 'stead of ol' Mel. Damn close, I'd say."

Rosanna turned to him. "How come I don't know about this marryin'? I ain't never heard of it til now?"

" Remember October in '16. Remember that dance? I was of a mind to take you? I figured you wanted me to?"

"Yes. So? Why didn't you?"

"War. Joe and me. We reported the next morning. So I couldn't. Went to France."

"You think that's an excuse?"

"Seemed like a good one at the time. I asked Mel to take you to the dance and look, ya'all got married, had four kids. The fairy tale never ends." Gavin was studying the pattern in the brick flooring of the platform. He said, "Joe and me spent the evening with Ma. Lucky we did. 'Fore we got back she was dead. Influenza, I guess. It was our last time together. Course Joe never got back hisself."

"That was a plenty sad time, Garvin. I remember. I do. I went to the funeral with my folks and with Melvin. I'm so sorry."

"Thanks, Rosanna." He smiled at her. "Bottom line was I held Momma's hand and Mel held yours and you two lived happily ever after...in Iona."

Rosanna giggled aloud. "Yeah, that's how it was all right. Happily ever after in Iona."

"Well, dear lady," Garvin stood up. "I suppose I better fill those cans, get to the post office and to the store and do those Tuesdays things I do so well."

"I suppose you should," Rosanna repeated. "Those damn cats won't live another day without you."

"I thought you were against swearin'?"

"That's not swearin'. I hate cats. That's the only kind there is." Rosanna looked up at him. "You doing all right, everything considered?Anything I can do for you?"

"Thanks, Rosanna. I'm fit as a fiddle. Me, the damn cats and the dog. We're takin' care of things."

"I can see that you are."

Garvin turned to leave and hesitated. "There is one thing," he said turning back to her, a grin forming on his whiskered cheeks.

"What's that?"

"There's that kiss."

Roseanna hesitated, staring at him. "What kiss?" she asked, suspecting a trick.

"That kiss," he repeated.

She stared, waiting for him to explain.

"You know, Rosanna, that kiss. The kiss by which all other kisses in the world are judged and are found wanting. If I hadn't gone to war, if I had taken you to that dance, I figure you and I would have shared that kiss; the very one I'm talking about. And all those folks in France, they wouldn't have died. Joe, he'd be here not stuck somewheres in Flander's Field. My mother would still be here. She wouldn't have died-- at least not then. That kiss. That's what it is all about. That's the cause."

"That's some kiss."

"Yes, and we'd have shared it."

"In your dreams. Buster Brown."

"Yes," he said. "Every night of every day." Garvin tipped his hat, smiled and walked down the platform.

Rosanna giggled to herself, watching him lift the empty five gallon cans, one in each hand, carrying them toward the hand pump. *He's sixty-five*, she thought. Way down the tracks she heard the whistle and could see the tiny black dot that was the engine, white smoke pouring from the stack. She watched it grow bigger and bigger until it was standing in front of the station, steam pouring from the boiler vent, a thin trail of smoke leaving the stack. The engineer waved at her as he always did, then looked down the platform at the conductor assisting passengers-- waiting for the signal that would send the train on its way.

The following Tuesday Rosanna Porter was sitting on the green bench where she had been waiting for ten minutes.

"Afternoon, Rosanna."

She looked up to see Garvin sitting himself down beside her, the bench creaking as it accepted his weight.

He said, "I see it's Tuesday and here you are. Nice to see you again, Rosanna."

"Hello," she said, looking at him. "I have something to say to you."

She could hear the train whistle from five miles away as it came through Sheep Canyon. It always did that. "Train's coming so I better be quick," she said, pausing, "in saying what I've got to say."

"All right," he said. "Go ahead. Let's hear what you got to say."

"Don't rush me, Garvin. I've been thinking this over." She glanced at him, then stood up, so close she could have touched his knee with her fingers. "It's about that kiss," she said. "The one you told me about. Remember?"

"I...."

"Please do not interrupt." She sat down primly on his lap. A look of astonishment came across his face. "I have decided to share 'the kiss' with you. I decided we have to stop people from dying. And from getting lost in France. Yes, that, too. And for one other reason. You were supposed to take me to the dance in 1916. I was eighteen. That's forty-six years ago. I don't think I can wait that long for you to ask me to another dance without you going off to war or falling off a horse and breaking a leg. We have to stop the sadness and the dying. That's why I decided to share the kiss with you."

91

Rosanna kissed him, her arms around his neck, her lips on his. It wasn't hurried. It lingered a little. Finished, she looked at him, waiting, still sitting in his lap, her feet not touching the brick platform, her arms still around his neck.

"How was that?" she asked. "Was that what you expected?"

"No," he said, staring at her in disbelief, still feeling her lips on his, enjoying the fresh soap smell of her. "It sure as hell wasn't what I expected. And it ain't one I'm likely to forget."

"Are you happy with it?"

"I...sure ain't unhappy."

"Good. There's another thing." Rosanna was looking at him again with all her attention. She certainly had his. "Garvin, I have never ridden a train," she said, pausing.

"You haven't?"

She shook her head. She said, "So I bought two tickets. I want you to come with me."

"Where we going?"

"Billings."

"What are we doing in Billings?"

"We're going to find a Justice of the Peace. I'm so sorry, Garvin. I know I'm being forward. I can't wait for you to get around to it. I'm not sure how long that would take."

A few hundred feet south of the Kane Depot the train was approaching. It had slowed down. He could see the engineer, his head out the window of the engine.

92

Garvin smiled. He looked at her. In front of the couple the train came to a stop, steam billowing from the tortured brake cylinders and steam vents, the drivers seizing. It came to a halt. Down the platform the conductor stepped from the first passenger car and looked both ways.

Rosanna Porter stood and looked at Garvin sitting on the bench. She waited for the noise to subside before finding her voice. She said to him, "Coming?"

Garvin Porter rose to his feet without a word and followed her toward the string of passenger cars and the conductor unloading passengers. Rosanna glanced toward the engineer. He was smiling down at her from his perch. She waved. He waved back as he always did.

Garvin and Rosanna Porter sat in the front of the second passenger car. Garvin had the window because Rosanna didn't want it. The train had been moving west for twenty minutes. Halfway back a young couple were sitting together, talking. They'd gotten on the train in Greybull. Now, except for Garvin and Rosanna, they had it all to themselves.

"Ok, ok. We gotta move," the young woman said to her companion. She spoke in a whisper loud enough to be heard by him over the rattling of the moving passenger car.

"Why?" Her companion responded.

"Ok, ok. Do you see that old couple?"

He looked up. "Yeah," he answered. "What about them?"

"Ok, ok, she's sitting in his lap!'

"So?"

"Ok, ok. She kisses him. See? They did it again. Every time she does she says, 'How was that one?' He says, 'Pretty damn good, Rosanna. But it ain't as good as that first one. That first one was the kiss. That's the one we'll remember.' Ok. Ok, so then she says, 'Do you think we ought to stop looking?' He says, 'No. We might find another that might be better. You never know.' Then she up and kisses him again. They have done that ten times. Maybe eleven. It is just gross. We have to move. I might throw up."

"Lilly, you're eavesdropping."

"I ain't." She paused, thinking about his statement. "Ok. Ok, well, I guess I am a little. But Jimmy, it's gross. They are so old. And they are right there in front of us. I can't help it. It's not like I can plug my ears or anything. We gotta move, ok?" She paused. "Right now!"

Jimmy looked at the old couple. "Hey lady," he yelled above the noise, trying to make sure she heard him. "What's the kiss you're looking for? The one you two can't seem to find?"

Rosanna raised her head and fixed the young man in her gaze, judged him to be in his mid-twenties. She paused before she answered, choosing her words with care. "That kiss," she said, "that kiss is the kiss by which all other kisses are judged."

Rosanna looked at Garvin, then back to the young man. Garvin was smiling, listening. She looked back at what she considered a "sure enough" youngster. "Once you have experienced it, all others pale in comparison. Everyone gets one. Just one." She raised her index finger for emphasis. "But you better be careful," she warned. "People die when you don't find it right away. Lots of people die. And they get lost in France and nobody can find them. Not ever." She shifted her gaze back to Garvin and kissed him on the lips, holding the embrace. Finished, she pulled away from him, still close.

"What about that one?" she asked Garvin.

"I like that one. It was especially good."

"Me, too. I liked that one."

Jimmy slid down in his seat beside Lilly. "Did you hear that?" he said quietly. "Did you hear what she said? People die if we don't find 'that kiss.' That's what she said. People die. And we're entitled to one. Everyone get's one. Us, too. I think we better start looking, don't you? No telling how many lives we could save, we find that kiss." He laughed and winked at Lilly.

"Get out of here," Lilly said, shaking her head in disbelief. " I ain't gonna look for no kiss with you. Not on no train."

"You sure?" Jimmy asked. "People die."

Cowboys at Roundup

96

CHAPTER 11

CASE OF A MISSING COW
AND A CAN OF BEER

Preface

They came in the fall of the year. They came in mid-October before the first snow fell above the timberline and after the first frost, and always after the third crop of hay was in the stack, curing. They came because there were no barbed wire fences and because a cow hardly ever stays put. In the summer months some cows would wander twenty miles chasing a stem of sweet grass and a sip of water. Sometimes a few walked off the mountain, restless, sometimes into the next county. More often than not they wandered just down the creek, over the next rise. They came because grazing was open and only a well affixed brand brought a man's stock home in the fall. Sometimes a hot running iron prevented even that but that's another story. Mostly they came because everyone must carry his own weight; because it was expected.

There were folks from out on Crystal Creek, from Crooked Creek, Sage Creek, Davis Creek, Layout Creek, the Dry Head and Shell Creek and riders from over the mountain as far away as Dayton on the Sheridan side. Represented were big outfits

97

with a couple thousand head and small rancheros with a couple of hundred cows and a few bulls. Crow riders came looking for cows that had wandered from the Basin pasture and the Bull Elk. They came from as far away as Fort Smith, Hardin, and St Xavier. These cowhands were tall, rangy fellows more a part of a horse than not. Not sixty years before, these mountains and meadows had all been claimed by their progenitors , and that of the Teton Lakota. Now no one knew for sure who the mountain belonged to but they came anyway for the cows and because it was done. It is the way it was.

It was a motley crew. Some short, some tall, and everything in between. They came on horseback, spurs and jinglebobs a jingling. They came wearing bat wing chaps and woolies, ten gallon hats and wool caps. They came clean shaven and bearded, soft spoken and rowdy, drunk and sober. At any one time there were as many as thirty riders, sometimes more. They worked from before sun-up until after dark. It was their business. It was their life. It was expected.

The mountain range encompassed over forty sections of grass and timber with plenty of places for a cow to hide, and hide they did. The gathering took days that often ran into weeks. Every rider was needed.

Once gathered, cows were separated by brand. Then the cows were allowed to stand, left to search for their calves amidst the mass confusion and disruption by bawling for them. There was a cacophony of sounds: bellowing cows, calves crying *for their mothers and milk, calves crying in pain as their hides were branded, their horns and gonads forcefully removed. There were men cursing, laughing, grumbling over a dozen perceived wrongs and at the end of the day happy doing what they were doing and being what they were. To the man there was no other life, no other reason for living. Not that they would say it or even think about it but that is the way it was.*

Red came to round-up because he was missing a Hereford Bull, three cows, and their unbranded yearling calves. One of the cows was a Holstein milk cow, easy to see and identify. These cattle had wandered out of Hannon's Cooley and mixed with the Association herds. Red suspected a couple of cows were somewhere around Old Gold City, maybe down on Porcupine Creek or Bald Mountain. Who knew? That's what he'd been told and that's where he found them last year. The fact was a cow given to wandering...wanders.

He located his Bar S cows as the herds were gathered and worked. One by one he moved them down on to Porcupine Creek and then returned to help the others, working until the job was done. That's where they were until the South Ranch outfit saw fit to help Red keep his cows separated.

He found out what they had done as the Round up finished. A beefy South Ranch Hand found him working cows with Indian hands from Fort Smith and a fellow named Flury. The South Ranch hand sought him out as he dragged a yearling in to be branded. After the bull calf had been thrown to the ground the rider, wearing a red cotton shirt, sidled up to him riding a roan horse.

"Say, Red," he said. "We found those cows of yours down on Porcupine Creek and moved them this side of the Jaws. Put them in with those of ours, we did. Thought you'd want to keep them separate from these here Crow cows. What you got that Holstein for, anyway?"

"Why'd you do that?" Red responded, irritated. "I was figuring on pushing them over on to the Cooley to winter them. It took me two weeks to find them and get them separated. I surely wish you hadn't. What the hell were you folks thinking?"

"Well," the man said slowly, taken back by Red's disapproval, "We did that so they don't get confused with that Association bunch and these here Indian cows. They were startin' to wander so we shoved them over with ours. They'll be all right. We'll round them up for you when you're ready."

Red wasn't so sure. But it had already been done. Nothing much he could do about it. Not now.

"All right," he finally said. "Thanks for letting me know." He acknowledged the speaker with the wave of his hand, then watched him as the rider retreated to the cook wagon. Red shook his head in disapproval then rode the bay away from the branding fires, dragging his lariat behind his horse to catch another yearling. Another thirty head and they'd be done. As the bay moved toward the herd Red coiled his rope.

This is going to be trouble, he thought. *Seven head in the middle of fifteen hundred. All the same breed except for the Holstein. What were they thinking?*

Toward the end of the day, he found the rep for that South Ranch outfit.

"I'll be leavin' tomorrow," Red informed him. "I want to move those cows of mine back toward the Cooley. Your man, Harold, that beefy fellow wearin' a red shirt, he told me you folks had pushed them over with that bunch of yours." Red said all of that before he realized the Rep was drunk and probably hadn't understood a word he'd said.

The rep's words came slowly and confirmed his suspicion.

"He did. Did he?" A pause. "We'll be a givin' you a hand." Another pause. "Finding them again. Myself, I saw that Hereford bull this morning. Twice I saw him. Two times."   A long pause. "And one of them cows. I saw one of them. Shouldn't be no trouble finding them. I don't think. Be right there and I'll do it. We'll help you find them. Sure as hell. When did you want them?"

Red had to listen carefully to understand what the man said; his speech was so slurred.

Contrary to their promises, they didn't help. Long into the evening the South Ranch hands stayed close to the grub wagon, drinking. One or two were down on Porcupine Creek watching the herd but they were drinking too. Whatever they were, "help" wasn't one of them. Something about their manner was unsettling. Something wasn't right; they started

101

laughing every time they saw him coming. Some just looked away not saying anything. The hair stood up on the back of Red's neck. Something was wrong.

The next day as he was waiting for the promised "help," Red rode through the South Ranch herd twice, taking his time. Mostly the cows looked underfed and seemed restless. He would have ridden through them a third time except one of the South Ranch riders met him.

Without greeting Red he started speaking loudly as though Red couldn't hear.

"We'll get them for you, Red," he said. "Not to worry yourself now. Hear me. We'll get them for you." The rider nearly fell off his horse. Somehow he managed to stay on.

"You can't do it alone," he said. "Damn fool to try. We'll give you a hand this afternoon. How about, tomorrow morning? We're doing a little celebratin' tonight."

What the rider really meant was he didn't want Red looking for his stock amongst the South Ranch herd. Odd thing was Red didn't see any of his stock, not even the Holstein cow. That one would have stood out plain as a knot on a bald head but the black and white cow wasn't to be found. Red began to doubt that his cows had been turned in with the South Ranch herd.

The evening and the next morning came and went without any of the promised help. Red waited. A South Ranch hand found him just after noon of the second day. He was a skinny rider with a blue shirt.

Some of his buttons were missing. He was bleary eyed and unshaven.

"Them cows of yourn," he said, "don't you worry yourself none, Red. We'll bring them off the mountain for you. And you can have them when we get them to Kane. We'll be startin' in a day or so. We're lettin' them settle before we start pushin' 'em off the mountain. It'll be a day or so," he said, repeating himself. "Maybe six or seven days. We'll have them at the railroad stock yard. Right down there at Kane. You can pick them out there. Should be no problem."

Doubtful, Red realized he wasn't being given any choice in the matter. Red left the separating flats without the Hereford bull, without the three cows, the Holstein, and without their yearling calves. He left with the repeated promises of "We'll get them for you" and "Not to worry" ringing in his ears.

I know, Red had thought, *as soon as you finish that last can of beer...and the two that follow that "last" one. And as soon as you can stand up. And as soon as you can walk without falling down. And as soon as you can get some help--sometime after that "helper" fellow finishes his "last" bottle and his "last" can.*

Red knew something else. He knew that anytime you're being told not to worry. Start. His Bar S cows were gone. Maybe lost in fifteen hundred head of milling stock...all belonging to....South Ranch. Maybe not.

I could find them myself, he thought. *But with no help. Probably not. I'll never see them again.*

103

Especially the yearlings. Not a chance in hell, he thought. *It's by design, all by design. Those three yearlings! Simply lost. No way to find them. Not without a lot of time and some help. Not separated from their mothers. They'd just bawl for three, four days and that would be it. They're gone. Lost, and there isn't a damn thing I can do about it. And those "so in sos" know it.*

Riding off the mountain, Red knew four things. He knew the South Ranch hands would drive their cows off the mountain. All fifteen hundred head. He knew that they'd hold them in the railroad stock yards at Kane. He knew that they'd work them while they had them in the stock yard, separating those they'd keep from those they'd sell. And he knew they'd separate the mavericks so they could mark and brand them. It would take them awhile because they'd be drinking. And he knew his stock wasn't among them.

As Red suspected and had been told, that is exactly what happened. Fifteen hundred and forty-six head were in the railroad stockyards one week later. Red was there, waiting. He was there for three days and not once did he come across the Bar S bull nor any one of the Bar S cows.

The South Ranch hands were still bent on drinking that "last" can of Budweiser. Chasing it with that "last" bottle of Johnny Walker Red. Still drinking the Big Horn Basin dry.

In their inebriated states they said to Red, "We looked for those Bar S cows of yours. We figured that Dayton outfit got ever' damn one, them thievin' sonstabitches. Maybe those folks from over Shell way. Probably mixed with theirs. We sure as hell looked, Red. Couldn't find them."

Every time one of the South Ranch hands got close to Red they repeated the same refrain. It got old and monotonous and Red knew it was a damn lie. Red thought it a miracle that they did any work. After all they spent most of their time drunk and when they weren't drinking they were taking a piss.

Red verified their statements. His cows just weren't there. Not one. *Odd,* he thought.

Red decided he'd had enough and told them so, told them he'd be leaving for home. The South Ranch outfit reassured him again.

"You know we looked, Red. Sure as hell." They said that, then laughed and snickered, nodded knowingly among themselves.

The big one with the scar on his face asked for another beer.

"Would you like one, Red? Have a beer with us. Sure too bad 'bout that bull," he said. "A good one that. And those cows. What do you need with a milk cow any way?" He laughed again, taking a long swig, smacking his lips, then took another. He stared at Red, smiling as if he had forgotten what he was going to say.

"No, but thanks," Red said. He mounted the bay horse and rode home. He chuckled to himself.

Those boys sure must think I have less brains than a bent nail, he thought. *One hell of a joke they're playing.*

It was four in the morning of the next day that Red saddled the bay gelding. Quietly, he smoothed the hair on its rump, then tightened the cinch, tugging at the latigo, slowly taking up the slack. Somewhere, perhaps close by, a hoot owl voiced concern. There was more than one owl doing the talking. It was hard to tell how far away or how many there were. The horse expanded his chest against the cinch, holding it as long as he could before letting it slip out. Red tightened the cinch again until he was satisfied the saddle wouldn't slip.

He'd been awake and dressed for over an hour. Once awake he'd taken his time. He'd fried three slices of bacon and some sliced potatoes in a cast iron skillet before mixing in three hens eggs.

Finished eating he caught up the bay. Once in the saddle the bay was moving, urged into a trot by the rowels of spurs that hung from the underslung heels, hidden under batwing chaps. Overhead a shovel full of far flung stars lit the sage brush and greasewood with a dim, muted light. In the east there was not even the hint of dawn. The air was cold, each evening finding the mercury just below freezing, draping limb and blade in hoar frost. It was cold but not so much as to freeze water in a bucket. The days found the temperature in the low forties under mostly cloudless skies.

The stockyards of the Chicago, Burlington and Quincy railroad were three quarters of a mile away from his front porch. Not far for Red and the bay horse to travel. He wasted no time. The loading chutes and cutting corrals were littered with dark beer bottles, Budweiser cans and Johnny Walker Red whiskey bottles. Red paid little attention to the evidence of the October celebration. He had other things on his mind.

Quickly, Red opened the exterior gate and rode down the alley. Pens full of mostly Hereford cattle were on both sides. They watched him moving through their midst in the darkness. Some got up. Most were lying down. A calf bawled for its mother. Then another. The brandless yearlings were in a corner pen; thirty-four head of bull calves and heifers. Yearlings all. Red quickly cut out eleven head and drove them down the alley and outside, shutting the gate behind him without dismounting. A rooster crowed. Across the tracks a dog barked. Once outside Red kept the eleven head walking north, down the road away from the railroad corrals, their tracks lost amid those of the herd being driven in. A dim light was forming over the Big Horn Mountains forecasting a dawn sometime in the future.

Thirty-five minutes later Red had the yearlings in Frank Good's cutting corral, a rope in his hand and another hanging from a fence post. Just outside the gate a small fire burned vigorously heating four irons.

In the early morning Red worked the eleven head of spring calves, catching them one after another. First he caught a head and a front foot securing it to a pole. With the other rope he caught a hind foot, then he stretched the yearlings out on their right side between opposite corral poles. Pulling an iron from the fire he burned its ribs with the Bar S brand. After each was branded and if need be, castrated, he turned it loose into the hay fields with one hundred and fifty head of mother cows and their spring calves. Those yearlings were already branded.

Once finished Red spent the early morning washing dishes and cleaning the kitchen. He watched the sun come up and thought about the new yearlings grazing out in the hay fields thought how fortunate he was, eleven yearlings, seven of his cows having borne twins and all. What a miracle. He thought about the bull, the three cows and their calves that he'd lost to a bunch of drunks who knew so much.

He shook his head, chuckled to himself, then went out to milk his remaining milk cow that he "didn't" need, so he could drink milk he "didn't" want, and slop the hogs with the left over strippings that they probably "didn't" want either. What a hell of a note.

He never said a word.

The Jaws on the Big Horn Mountain

CHAPTER 12

BILL AND ME

1. WORK AND THE TRUE NATURE OF LIFE

Sitting bareback on seventeen hands of bay horse and looking back a number of years, I've got to say this: There is nothing lonelier then a Model A Farmall tractor sitting in the middle of a field of fresh-cut hay, the four banger of an engine quiet, the squeak of the side delivery silent, the beater no longer turning. Nothing at all as lonely.

In the summer of 1956 that tractor was pulling a red side delivery hay rake manufactured by International Harvester. Everything was red in the old man's fields. Except for the Johnny Poppers in everyone else's fields, nothing was John Deere green.

A windrow of hay, wet and limp from falling over the cycle bar, trailed behind that now stationary tractor that had pulled the rake. It was more or less a straight row. On that midmorning summer day the four cylinder engine was still warm; hot to the touch. Grease still hung to the tractor and rake bearings from being lubed mere hours before. The gas tank was three-quarters full; the top, wet where the fuel leaked out around the gas cap as it sloshed back and forth as the tractor had moved up and down the hay field. A Model A isn't a big tractor but it has sufficient power for a nine-year-old boy pulling a hay rake. It would have done the job Dad intended if I'd continued to sit on the tin seat, hands gripping the steering wheel, but that wasn't destined to happen.

It is easy to daydream guiding an Model A Farmall up and down the long windrows of a hayfield. It is easy to sleep, too. When I first started raking hay I was six. In October I'd be seven. It didn't take long for me to go to sleep dreaming that I wanted to be somewhere else. I didn't know where because I was too small to know there was a "some place" else. Somewhere in the middle of first cutting I went to sleep and drove tractor and rake through Harvey Nebel's barbed wire fence and almost into his irrigation ditch. I woke up before I had the front wheels parked permanently in the bottom of his ditch. I woke up because the tractor was bouncing like crazy as it climbed the ditch bank, nearly throwing me under the wheels.

Instantly, I was off the seat pulling on the steering wheel and pushing the clutch down as far as it would go before it could throw me. (I had to get off the seat. Otherwise, I couldn't push the clutch in all the way. That's what happens when you have short legs.) Once I took a look at the situation I figured I'd have to back up because going forward didn't look too promising. Harvey Nebel hadn't even cut his hay yet. Wouldn't do me or him any good to pull that rake through his stand up alfalfa just to turn around in his field and drive back across the ditch. Besides, I didn't want to explain all this to Dad.

Model A Farmall

Sitting on the very lip of the seat, I got the A tractor into reverse, backed up three or four times, and managed to get back in the hay field. I turned up field and took another swath of hay that my Dad had cut that very morning. For a while I kept going up and down those rows much more awake than I had been. But the sun was hot: the air was humid: bugs were buzzing: and I was getting a terrific tan. Already I was browner than that berry Eddie Arnold sang about on the five o'clock a.m. edition of the Omaha stock report. My going up and down that field didn't last long. It couldn't. Soon my head was bobbing like one of those bobble head dolls with full range of motion.

Eventually, sometime after my eyelids were threatening to beat me to death, I pushed the clutch in, took the tractor out of gear, crawled out onto the wheel, and jumped down to the earth. I left the tractor running because I couldn't start it by myself. So with it happily chattering above my head I crawled under it and went to sleep. For the next hour hay didn't get raked. The tractor did not run out of gas. I slept and didn't drive through Harvey Nebel's fence. At least not on that day. It was the summer of 1953.

Three years later, I did leave that very Model A sitting out in the middle of a fresh cut hay field midsummer 1956. It would have been within a day or two of June 19 because that is when Dad always started cutting hay. That year I was nine years old, planning on being ten in October. I left that tractor because Bill came riding up on a painted horse, leading a bay. Both horses were bareback, bridle only, no saddles, nothing to get in the way or slow us down. Bill was wondering why I was raking hay. I didn't know, so I shut the tractor off, climbed out on the rear tire, and jumped on the back of the bay horse. That was the last time I was on that Model A that summer.

And that summer, neither one of those horses gained a pound; they never stood still long enough. They were in the best shape ever. We never stopped riding, except, maybe, to sleep and go to church when I was absolutely forced into it. Mothers can bring a lot of pressure to bear when it comes to God, Jesus, eating breakfast and chores.

113

There were rules. Breakfast and chores were a requirement before I could get back on that kid's "damn" horse. I thought Bill was incredibly lucky. As far as I know his mom never made him go to church and everybody but Bill had chores. He was just different and lucky--mostly lucky, but I said that already. Sexy Rex in one respect was lucky like Bill: he also never had to go to church like the rest of us.

Everyone liked Bill. Mother thought him a "cute kid." Dad called him "Wild Bill." Even my sister thought he was okay. After all, he did hold her Double H 4H lamb for her at the County Fair in Basin. Dot Nebel thought Bill was a juvenile delinquent and that Mother was "certainly not using her head" letting me associate with him. "It could only lead to certain trouble. Lots of trouble," she said. By her edict, her Sexy Rex couldn't associate with the likes of Bill. But he couldn't do a lot of things that everyone else did. Mothers are that way. Mrs. Nebel claimed her Rex was going to be a Doctor or the President and that his reputation could not be sullied. Whatever that meant.

I don't know what happened to Dad the summer of '56. He sort of disappeared. He never said anything to me about that lonely Model A sitting in the hayfield. I know he finished raking the hay, although I never saw him. Occasionally he'd ask about the chores but the hogs were slopped, the milk-cow was juiced, the cows in the corral were fed, and their drinking water was pumped. I suspect he knew the answer before he asked the question. He seemed to know everything. As the summer wore on

114

into the beginnings of September he stopped asking altogether.

That day in June, Bill and I rode from the hayfield to the Big Horn River. Where else was there to go? The Big Horn had a crazy bridge. It was so high above the river that you couldn't jump off of it. You'd get killed. No one did that. It was tall because the engineers and surveyors who built it were anticipating the construction of the Yellowtail dam at Fort Smith seventy miles down river. Money hadn't even been appropriated for it but they were anticipating that it would be. They were a bunch of idiots, really. Probably educated some place like Yale, Harvard, or Penn State where they educate fools to work for the government. Turned out the high bridge was too low so they had to raise it. And the railroad? They had to move it to higher ground twice to keep the ties from getting wet from the planned lake. And the causeway? Too low. Had to be raised . . . twice.

There it is: Plaintiff's Exhibit A. Proof that a bunch of educated idiots with sharp pencils and no clue can only work for the government. Because they were so well qualified, the government hired them. Now you know who works for the government and you also know who shouldn't.

During the summers, Bill and I lived under the river bridge. We swam naked and often. Naked was the order of the day. We had to because the river water turned white J.C. Penney jockey shorts to a permanent dingy grey that even Tide and a cup of

Hay field Abandoned the Summer of 1956

Clorox bleach couldn't handle. Moms didn't care much for that particular color.

We had an everyday ritual. After swimming in the Horn we went to the Shoshone bridge which wasn't so high. It was a little over a mile away. A time or two we jumped off the piers into its cold water. The difference in the water temperature of the two rivers was about ten degrees. When it was ninety degrees in the shade it didn't make a lot of difference except it felt even colder. Once the river swimming holes had been explored, we went to the irrigation canal where it passed under Highway 14A to swim again. The canal passed under the highway and the current created a nice swimming hole and kept it washed out. Our average number of swims was five or six times a day.

Living at the confluence of two rivers and having a canal in your backyard had benefits. I learned to swim, my hair never dried. I got a nice tan, stayed cool, learned how to smoke, and discovered that nothing really was sacred except maybe horses, swimming, green apples, and the morning sun.

There were seven of us boys that tried to grow up together. In spite of ourselves most did. There was Sexy-Rex who, according to his mom, could not associate with Bill, and whose dad drove the school bus. Truth was he did anything he wanted to do regardless of his mom grooming him to be the next Doctor Tom Croft.

There was Larry who had to work because Ellises work and had a lot of pigs to feed. Plus that, his mom was the last postmaster in Kane and made hot chocolate to die for. I am not sure if Larry got religion but I went to Bible School with him in the basement of his church.

There was Bob, who could run around wild as long as his mom didn't find it necessary to exercise her "mom" authority to prove that she was mom. No one had any doubt of her status except, maybe, her. Cowboy Bob thought he was John Wayne and had me fooled. He looked plenty cool sitting on a horse looking stern, his bandanna wrapped tightly around his neck.

There was Bill, who I am not sure had parents. Whitey and Blanch were his dad and mom but were mere observers. He proved the validity of one invaluable rule: You can get away with anything, say anything, as long as you are smiling.

There was Johnny, whose dad made him work more than any of us, and was incredibly smart; he must have had an IQ of 180. Later, he met a girl named Jane and that, as they say, was all she wrote. John was gone.

There was Pete who spent his time and most of his life trying to be his cousin John. (Not the incredibly smart Johnny but John the football player.) Pete walked around sounding like a submarine about to surface and was particularly interested in the preacher's daughters. He often tried to impress upon Bill his physical toughness, his rowdy, "let's rumble" persona. That all came to a head when Pete tried to beat the hell out of Bill only to have Bill's Boxer dogs put him up a cottonwood tree. He'd still be there if Bill's dogs hadn't gotten old and died.

Lastly, there was me. I did have parents. Mother liked me so I got to do all the stuff she never knew about. The irony: she thought Bill was perfect. Not even Bill's mom thought that.

Of these seven, we all managed to grow up in Kane, Wyoming. At least we got older, except, maybe, Pete. He got himself killed, so he never had the chance to do a whole lot of growing up.

Me Standing in the Hay field - Joe Broscious Place

Bill leaving the kitchen

2. WATER AND BILL'S IMPERIAL NAVY

In August 1957 Bill found a canoe. I don't know where he got it. I guess he discovered it floating down the Shoshone below his house. Somehow we got it to the Big Horn River. It was too heavy to hand carry so we had to hitch a ride. Paint was peeling off its plywood sides. There wasn't anything to sit on except the bottom. It had structural cross pieces that kept the sides from meeting in the middle. Mostly it kept water on the outside and Bill and me sort of dry on the inside. It was long and hard to maneuver. No oars were available, so we pushed it around with poles furnished by the river. It was perfectly safe. There were no life jackets, therefore we couldn't drown. That's a rule.

Once we acquired the canoe we started looking for another. It was pure logic. If one is fun, two is more fun. The second water craft in Bill's armada just fell into our laps.

The first time we saw the flatboat it was tied to a rusted I-beam a hundred yards upstream from the monster bridge where the first old bridge stood. It had been removed. All that was left of that bridge was that I-beam jutting out of the ground. We borrowed that boat and had so much fun we borrowed it again. After the first borrowing we kept it. Whoever owned it must have thought they'd lost it. And they had. After all, the rope was no longer tied to the I-beam and the flatboat had disappeared. They probably thought it had pulled loose and drifted down the river, got lost in the Narrows or the canyon, or maybe it had floated clear to Fort Smith. Maybe it had. It was a nice boat. It was at least sixteen feet long, painted battleship grey, and came with two long green oars. In the evenings when we weren't using our "armada," we'd hide them in the brush that grew along the west bank of the river. We made them invisible so that we could keep them. It was the magic of the river.

If the original owners had looked several hundred yards downstream, they would have found Bill and I, in a shaded cove, sitting in the flatboat, naked, gnawing on green apples we'd borrowed from Chris Schatz, and smoking punk cigarettes. Every so often we'd jump in the river to cool off and keep the mosquitoes and deer flies at bay. Our horses would stand under leafy, cottonwood trees, reins tied to a limb, getting a much needed rest, switching their tails at flies, soaking up the shade and cooling down.

Given our diet, I can't say we gained any weight in the summer. In spite of our regimen, we still managed to grow taller by an inch or so. Bill, more than me. He was older and it was in the nature of things for him to grow taller before me. Fact is, he is still taller than me. I never caught up. But he's also still older by seven months and a big week. So I'm working on it, and I've got time. Bill, not so much.

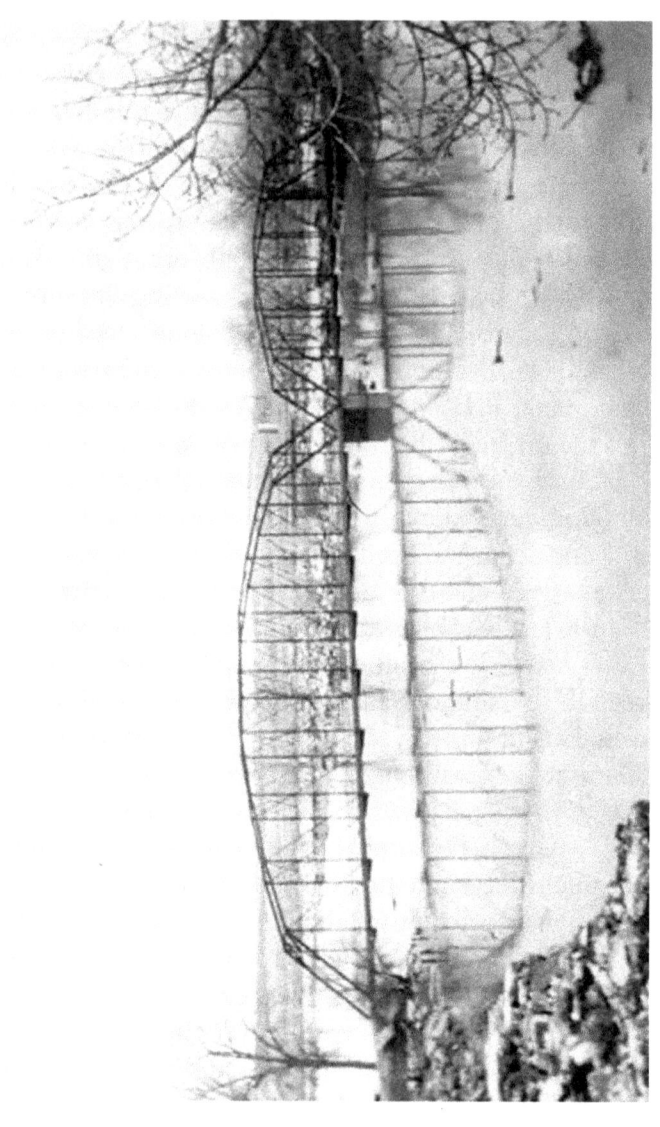

First Big Horn River Bridge that drove the ferry man
out of business

3. WHITE WATER AND COTTONWOOD TREES

When it was April, April was my favorite month. If it was May, I'd go with May. The last week in April meant the end of school was a month away. That ending day was an important day: May 22, 1957. Ice was no longer floating in either river. Baby calves were on the ground. The grass was greening up, as were the cottonwood and elm trees. I was ten. Bill had turned eleven February 22. For the five months following October 7, we had been the same age. As I said, he was older than me, but there was nothing we didn't know. Just ask. We could tell you. Besides we had two boats and two horses, two twenty-two rifles, and we could drive a pickup truck practically anytime we wanted.

In April, with the end of winter and the beginning of spring, we had a hellacious idea. We'd float down the Horn to the monster bridge in our canoe. As ideas go, it was incredible and we couldn't wait to try it out. What good is an idea if you can't do something about it? Frankly, there was no such thing as an idea that Bill didn't do something about. Clearly, he was gifted. It was his true talent.

Using the old man's 1954 Chevrolet pickup truck, we hauled the canoe upriver a ways. It turned out to be quite a way and the river bridge was an illusion of sorts. We thought it was a short distance because we could almost see the river bridge when we unloaded the canoe. So it wasn't far. Maybe three miles. But maybe not three miles. The river didn't run straight to the bridge. It was serpentine. It moved back and forth in long, lazy loops that extended the distance traveled three times the square root of a billion to a power of ten. We never thought about that. Our math skills were challenged, but only because we didn't use them. Fact is, we both did a better job with math than those government engineers and surveyors educated at Yale, Princeton, and Harvard who planned for bridges and railroads so incredibly well. And we were only ten. Well, in Bill's case: eleven.

On Monday we hauled the canoe upriver.

On Tuesday we got to the river about 5:30 in the afternoon. Maybe it was six, because Harvey Nebel and his yellow school bus had dropped me off at home. Every day, except when Harvey had to make an additional stop and throw someone off the bus, he'd let me, my sister, and, eventually, my brother, off ten minutes before five, just in time for me to listen to the *Lone Ranger* on the radio. That program drove my Dad crazy. He thought I should do the chores before I listened to the radio. Seldom was he home at 4:50 p.m. and I didn't ask. Me, the Lone Ranger and Tonto got along just fine.

We lived less than a mile from the river. Not far. It was early. The sun was still up. We weren't afflicted by daylight-saving time, nor were we afflicted by the idiots in Cheyenne and Washington that couldn't get over themselves because saving daylight was such an idea. As I said, that "maybe six" was real time and we had time. It was a day to be remembered. The sky was an incredible blue. Spring was everywhere. The air was warm, and it hadn't frosted for a week. It certainly was time to get after it. Bill and I hitched a ride to the river and to our canoe, to the long green oars, and to this incredible idea of canoeing down river to the monster bridge–a very short distance.

I got into the canoe first. I don't know why. It must have been because Bill was older. In getting in I moved forward, sitting up front in the middle with my long green oar. The inside of that canoe was dry. No water had even begun to leak inside. Bill got in last and pushed us out into the river with his oar. Immediately the current took us and we were gone, gone, gone. Sometimes I'd paddle. Bill guided, using the flat part of his oar in the water. Sometimes we'd both paddle. Consequently, we made the first loop in record time. It turned out that we hadn't moved a hundred yards downstream; the bridge was no closer than it had been when we started. But the sun was up and we had time.

Back then the Big Horn river bottom was incredibly peaceful; not so much now. Now, courtesy of those geniuses that graduated from Yale, it's mostly a dry mud hole. In the 50s it moved slowly through a forest of cottonwood trees. Sometimes it seemed as if it didn't move at all. But when it turned to go in the opposite direction, then, maybe not so much. Around the bends it sped up and the current went crazy. Bill was yelling "paddle, paddle, paddle" and I was. Somehow the front

127

became the back and the back, the front, and the canoe swamped itself and was full of water. We had to get to shore to dump it out.

In retrospect, I remember Dad telling me that when he was a kid the river took people: that every year some "good swimmer" drowned and was buried in the Iona cemetery. That was another thought that Bill and I had never had. Fact was, it was our river. It was our canoe. We had no life jackets. So what's the problem?

After cursing and swearing like troopers fresh from some foreign war that George Washington didn't want the country involved in, we put the canoe back into the river and made the second loop. It was just like the first. "Incredible." "Terrific." "Unimaginably cool," and a whole number of positive affirmations that mothers find "uncool." Trouble was, the monster bridge was still no closer. But the sun was still up and we had time. Lots of time.

The bend in the third loop was trickier. Bill yelled, "paddle, paddle, paddle" and again I did, but the end still turned out to be the front and vice versa. We swamped it. An oar dropped into the water. We tried to get it, but a single oar could not paddle a canoe fast enough to catch the first. We thought about jumping in to rescue it but the Big Horn water in April is a whole lot of cold and we were already more than a little wet. The river water was snow runoff and deep, so we lost that oar. Bill swears I lost it. I know he lost his because I still had mine. I'd plucked it out of the water.

By this time, the sun was no longer in the sky. Dark was chasing daylight into dark shadows. Stars were decorating the April heavens. Our clothes were wet and damp and the bridge was still a million miles away. When we turned following the river as it bent back, this time on the far east side of the river bottom, there was the bridge, right where we left it. The difficulty was it appeared no closer.

We made the fourth loop. After that I lost count of loops because it was dark and it was late. We decided to park the canoe and come back for her later. We knew where we were. Lost we were not. We knew how to get home. A chill had returned to the April air making it feel a little like March. We were hungry, and quitting seemed a good idea. Parents do tend to get a little edgy when their boys are out after dark in April, riding the river, in a canoe.

It was pleasant enough. The sky was full of night birds flitting about chasing bugs. The owls were talking among themselves. Coyotes were yapping. Frogs were singing. Crickets were rubbing their legs together like mad. In this cacophony of sound, we started walking west because west was the direction of home. There were no roads to make it easy. We fought skunk brush, sage brush, grease wood, short cottonwood and tall cottonwood. In the dark everything stood in the way and everything seemed much bigger than it is in daylight. Our wavering, convoluted path took us right through Bischoff's bull pasture. Not that we knew that at the time, for the direction we trod was just the shortest way home. Besides, we hadn't thought about what lived in bull pastures.

We heard bulls before we saw bulls. One, in particular, was filling the night with deep throaty bellowing, letting the world know that he was the bull to deal with. The reasons: there were pregnant cows in September, and to announce that no other bull could possibly compare with him. He pretty much had me convinced. His caterwauling caused us to move a little quicker–run, even. In our hurry we crossed an open park, a meadow of some size. And there that big, black bastard was. He was crossing the same open meadow, bellowing, trumpeting, moving right toward us. Bill started to run. Me, too. Bill was much quicker than I but I became quicker by the second. And that bull was looking to be much quicker than the both of us.

Fortunately for Bill and me, there was a cottonwood tree in the middle of the bull pasture and meadow. Fortunately, it wasn't too far away and the bull was on the other side. Unfortunately, the bull was closer to the tree than either of us wanted. Bill reached the tree first and was up it. Absolutely no one climbs a tree, any tree, quicker than Bill, and in those days no one ran faster than Bill. I reached that tree in a clear second place finish and had no idea how I was going to get up it but I felt inspired. A two thousand pound bull can provide plenty of inspiration.

In spite of all that pending inspiration, I never climbed that tree. I swear Bill reached down out of the top, grabbed my wrist, pulling me out of harm's way with that bull sniffing the bottom of my J.C. Penney Super Keds. There we sat perched securely in the upper branches for the next two hours with that bull stomping around the base of that short cottonwood. Every so often he'd pause, sniff the air, bellow, trumpet, then continue to pace around the tree. There is nothing like a bull bellowing at the base of your tree to liven your dreams with sheer terror. Not that we were asleep, but we should have been. It was that late.

Somewhere a little after O-dark thirty the bull lost interest. It was about the time we thought we'd be sitting up in the upper branches forever, starving to death. After the bull had wandered about thirty yards away, we climbed down and ran for our lives.

It was after 11:00 p.m. when I made it home minutes shy of midnight. Standing on the porch I knew I'd never be able to explain what had happened. Dad was still awake when I went inside. He glanced up from reading a weathered book with a broken spine, looked me over, and told me that we ought not to canoe on school days. On that occasion he made it a new rule; he repeated it several times: No canoeing on school days. I was good with it. I guess school was pretty important to him. Thank God he didn't ask for an explanation. I didn't have one.

Cal Kuchler and tunnel he worked on in Cascade County, Montana. Cal saved a man's life when he caught on fire from an oil torch during construction

4. A CAR

Horses are good. Wheels, however, are the true ticket to freedom. It's an immutable rule, a law cast in concrete and cured for a thousand years.

I was eleven when Cal Kuchler asked my mother if I could help him put a new roof on the brick school house in which he lived. She said yes and told me to do it; thus I was volunteered. What else was I going to do? Except for Cal, no one lived there. Once it had educated the kids from Kane and Iona. Dad had attended its bleak halls for eight grades and graduated.

Cal Kuchler was a crazy guy, older than dirt, and tall. Maybe he wasn't tall, but I was short, and that made him tall. Besides he found a bleached skull at the base of Low Mountain with a bullet hole in the forehead; he owned a ten gauge shotgun with scrolls etched into the barrel; he lived in a the biggest building in Kane, with its own stage, swings and bell. He didn't have a telephone so every time he rang the bell people would go to the school house to see what was wrong. Nothing ever was.

On Monday of the appointed day, he and I climbed the inside ladder to the bell housing and stood on the broad expanse of roof. Cal had in mind to nail new asphalt shingles to a tarred roof that really needed more tar. It was the wrong thing to do and I knew that, but it was Cal's roof, Cal's shingles and Cal's school house. What was I to say? I was

133

only eleven. So we started the project. But it was even more wrong than just shingles where tar should be. Cal wanted to start at the top and lay the shingles moving toward the bottom. Anyone and everyone except Cal knew that it was required to start at the bottom of the roof and work up, laying the new singles in rows. Otherwise the tops of the shingle nails aren't covered and the roof invariably would leak much better than it had ever leaked before.

I mentioned this to Cal but he thought I was eleven years old and didn't know what I was talking about. I was easily convinced and for the next week assisted him in laying shingles in the wrong direction. It is an understatement to declare Cal's roof really leaked, really well, after that job was finished. Later, Cal plugged the new holes with tar, which is what he should have done in the first place.

In return for my assistance in injuring the roof to the old school house he wanted to know if I wanted his car. The roof leaked. But from a purely aesthetic point of view the watermarks left in the plaster ceilings were something to behold. Michelangelo could not have designed a more colorful ceiling. It looked like a road map to an island in a choppy sea. I did not have an attack of conscience for accepting his car.

The car was something. In front of the school house, sitting on blocks, was a 1932 Model A Ford, two door coup, with a flathead V8. It wasn't running. The tires were not flat only because they weren't sitting on the ground.

Dad and I pumped the tires up (17 inch rims) and pulled it home behind his '54 Chevrolet pickup truck with its straight six, whose crankcase held nine quarts of 10W-30. I sat behind the wheel and steered. It was the first time I ever owned a car. It was a pretty big deal.

Bill and I got it to run by spending fifty-seven cents on a flexible fuel hose. Before we made that expenditure, we switched carburetors with some other wreck. The working model was a single throat job. Luckily, the breather element with an oil bath, fit. We obtained some sixteen inch wire wheels from somewhere. I do not remember who donated those rims. Obviously, the car we removed them from no longer had need of them. We acquired a six-volt battery from Dad's Farmall "H" farm tractor.

Having done all of that, we pushed it down the hill behind the house and, to our amazement, it started. Starting it, listening to all eight cylinders popping, made us aware that the engine block, where the radiator hose slid over the metal hose attachment, had a four-inch crack that ran parallel to the ground. It leaked Prestone. Not knowing that it wouldn't work, we pounded the crack full of a greased towel, using a screw driver as an insertion/compaction tool. Thus, the leak was plugged. The engine ran cool, and we were off.

The '32 Ford, according to Cal's last registration was a Model A. According to everyone who looked at the flat head V8, it was a model B. It didn't matter because we never licensed it. It wasn't licensed until 2011 when Grace Ann made the vehicle legal. Before that she spent a bazillion dollars replacing the flat head with chrome, a new engine, a new roof, a new everything--but that is another story.

Bill and I lived in that car and that car was lucky to have survived us. Conversely we were lucky to have survived it. It had its quirks. Around eighty it started to shimmy. At that speed it shook like crazy even on asphalt. It wasn't so bad on a dirt road because dirt roads are bumpy and it was hard to tell exactly what was shaking and what was not. Fortunately we didn't go that slow all of the time but we did go everywhere there was to go. To the west, that meant about nine miles nearly to Lovell; on the east we went to Five Springs and Cottonwood Canyon; on the north, clear to Dry Head Creek, and south, to the Kane Caves. It was necessary to park it on a hill because the starter motor was problematic and didn't always start the engine.

The first major modification of the exterior occurred in Minnie Gams' front yard and the road behind her house. We'd gone to see exactly where that road led. On the way back it started to hail. These were not normal ice crystals. Indeed, the sky was dropping huge softball sized projectiles. The banging came from all over and all around us in a popping cacophony of ice explosions. Pop. Pop. Pop. Bang. It was like a string of firecrackers exploding, punctuated once in a while by an M-80. The volume was turned all the way up. Jamming the accelerator clear to the floor, we tried to outrun it. It didn't help much. The thunder was rolling; the ice grenades were blasting away, stealing the life from all things living.

Henry Ford had designed the car with a structural weakness. The roof was an over laying of thick canvass covering chicken wire. The cloth and wire were supported on oak cross members held together with wood screws. Ice balls were busting through it with impunity. One hit the dog on the head, a punishment that he did not see coming and did not especially care for. So here we were flying down the dirt road, navigating through the ruts and rocks, ice balls busting around us like they were fired from machine guns, the dog yelping, the engine roaring, and hail pounding the roof and hood. To save ourselves we pulled into Minnie's front yard, seeking safety under a cottonwood tree. Leaves and branches were falling all around us, the dog was still barking, trying to escape the car, the engine was running, and we were laughing. It was great. The roof had holes in it. Afterwards, it was sort of a convertible. We could see blue sky through the roof from the front seat. It hadn't been that way before.

We took a trip in the '32 Ford to the Kane Caves. My red-headed younger brother was in the back seat with our guns: .22s fully loaded. We were looking for a bottle, a can, a rabbit: something to kill. It was an incredible day. On the way back that changed. We were not speeding. The car was going five miles an hour on the county road, if that. Bill was driving and he wanted to change gears. Normally the clutch would be pushed in with the left foot. Normally. Normal was abnormal with Bill. For some reason only known to Bill and God, he pushed in the clutch with his left hand. It is hard to see over the dash with your head down on your knees and your hand almost to the floor. It is impossible. He didn't mean to but he pulled the wheel.

Off the road we went. The wheels on the right side dropped down precipitously. The wheels on the left followed. Over and over we rolled. The drop was only fifteen feet on a forty -five degree incline. The car came to a standstill sitting upside down. Glen had a knot on his head, the guns didn't discharge, the door was bent back, the roof was a little closer to the floor board and the engine was merrily running. Bill was now sitting on the roof. He reached up and switched the engine off, flipping the toggle switch.

There was dust that hadn't been disturbed in thirty years falling all over us. We weren't sure we weren't dead, or if our legs and arms weren't broken, or worse, whether we were carless. Bill slipped out the bent driver's door. I crawled out the window. My brother sat on the bottom of the roof, the seat above his head, nursing this huge knot on his head. I remember thinking Mother would not be too happy about that knot.

Bill and I pushed the car over upright and onto its wheels. I don't know how we did that. It didn't seem heavy. It didn't even seem unusual. After thinking about it, I can only conclude that the adrenaline was pumping like crazy. How else can you explain two eleven-going-on-twelve year-old boys pushing a vehicle sitting on its top onto its wheels? When did that ever happen? I had trouble picking up a five-gallon pail of water and hefting a hundred-pound bale of hay. Those were heavy! But the car? Light as a feather.

Good fortune shined on us. Fifteen minutes later, George Ellis came driving along the county road. He was so taken with the image of Bill, my younger brother and I standing by our car in this off-road hole that he nearly joined us, coming within inches of driving off the embankment. George's head was poked out his pick-up window, his mouth wide open in amazement. It is a wonder he even saw us. We were twenty feet off the road, but the top of the car was ten feet below the road surface. Fortunately he saw us. To rescue us, Mr. Ellis got his Cat and made a road off the county road. We started the '32 up and were back in business.

With my brother once again sitting in the back seat accompanying our weapons of choice, we were off and gone. Behind us, as seen through the slightly bent rear-view mirror, George Ellis was standing in the middle of the county road, his Cat behind him idling, with this incredible look on his face. We certainly thanked him for rescuing us. It wouldn't be the last time. Larry had a great dad. We all agreed on that point of fact.

If my mother had known where we went, how far we went, and the impunity with which we traveled, she would have thought that car was a bad idea. For example, Bill and I were driving on the Iona side of the Shoshone with the idea of seeing how Johnny Schneider was doing. If Larry had to work, you could depend on Johnny working three times as hard and as long. But we never knew positively, so we went to see him.

We were riding along on the county road going north. Charley Scheeler was going south, driving his pick up truck. It was Bill's turn to drive. He was doing a good job as far as I could tell. The closer Charley got the closer Bill got to the middle of the county road. Closer, closer, closer. Bill skillfully put the right front fender a quarter of an inch from the side of Charley's pick-up.

Whoosh. We were by him. Charley came to a crazy stop, jumped out onto the running board of his truck and started shaking his fist and other things at us. That experience gave definition to the word "funny."

Charley Scheeler, bless his cranky heart, called the Highway Patrol, bent on having us arrested or shot. I think he preferred shot. We know because on our way back from watching Johnny work we saw the Highway Bull cruiser driving down the county road in front of us. Undoubtedly, Officer John Hampton was at the wheel with his chest full of badges and authority. Of course we stopped, waited, then went on to torment Charley Scheeler once more. My car never was arrested.

The Scheeler game of chicken was my first quasi-brush with law enforcement. Bill was much more careful in that respect than I. He'd been threatened with the Worland Boy's School and he

140

tried to do the Brer Rabbit thing and "lay low" in the presence of all things official.

The second time I met authority distinguished by badges and guns was in front of the Lovell Elementary school at the school bus stop. At the end of the school day as we were boarding Harv's yellow school bus, we noted Officer John Hampton. He was parked, sitting in his Wyoming Highway Patrol Cruiser in front of the bus. Harvey Nebel indicated to me, then Bill, that we were to have the privilege of riding home with the highway patrolman and, conversely, not his school bus.

Harvey took a great deal of pleasure in informing Bill and me that we had these special travel arrangements. His glee had some basis in fact and tradition. It was Harvey's purpose in life, written into his job description, to throw Bill off his school bus. He did it multiple times; ten to the power of nine. I had the privilege of receiving the full glare of Harvey's ire several times but not nearly as many as Bill. Bill, to this day, holds the record. As far as I can remember the only kid of the bunch that didn't get thrown off the bus was Sexy Rex, but he was Harvey's son. Politics and nepotism at the age of eleven. What can you do?

Officer Hampton kept his black and white cruiser shiny. At his invitation I got in the front seat and Bill, the back. We did this in front of the entire school with everyone watching. All the way home I kept wondering how Mother was going to react to me riding with Officer Hampton. I can say this. We got home sooner than those who rode with Harvey and I didn't get thrown off the bus. Neither did Bill. We were delivered to our front door step. Officer Hampton was good about doing that and we were most appreciative.

Why did we have this privilege? It seems that some idiot, apparently someone that was eventually hired by the government, was shooting out the railroad warning lights on Highway 14A, and was doing so about a half-mile from my house. There are all kinds of stupid and those inane bastards were well acquainted with them all.

Bill immediately told the highway patrolman that he knew nothing about it and that he hadn't done it. When it came my turn to answer the patrolman's questions, I said, "I didn't do it. I don't know who did it," and, "If I did know I wouldn't tell you."

Bill was crawling under the seat, practically begging for mercy. From the front seat, facing Officer Hampton, I could see him waving his hands, telling me to shut up. The next morning Bill lectured me on the formal etiquette of speaking to police officers.

"You are stupid even if you were telling the truth. Stupid," he said.

That's what Bill said. He's right. Bill became a cop, a deputy sheriff, a police chief, and for all I know, a U.S. Marshal. Even at eleven years he knew copspeak. The truth was we never shot out the railroad lights. We figured it was someone from Lovell. Turned out we were right.

Bill had cause for concern. Parents and grownups in general thought evil of him. It might have had something to do with fighting. In grade school Pete and Bill beat the hell out of each other at least every other day. Day in and day out would find Pete and Bill in Mrs. Baird's office getting the paddle. They were certainly good at fighting. They threw actual punches, ripped the pockets off of each other's shirts, bloodied each other's noses, cussed. I thought Bill was better, but Pete didn't know it. Physically, he was bigger so they went at it. It was a requirement in establishing the true pecking order. The irony was that they liked each other and were good friends. The end result of this activity was that people saw Bill, but not me. Grownups never saw me. This selective blindness was repeated often. For example, Chris Schatz rented the little Joe Brocisous farm. It was between my house and the Big Horn river and it had an apple tree. They were good apples, too. Bill and I stopped there frequently. Chris knew it. As luck would have it, he never got any apples

It was only once, but we got ourselves caught stealing his apples. We saw him coming a long time before he reached us. We knew we'd been caught but we ran as fast as we could to my Dad's pick-up truck, intent on escaping down the open highway. We were seated before Chris got to us. Trouble was the truck didn't start and our escape was thwarted.

Chris got out of his truck slowly like he was Bat Masterson and was about to kill somebody. He walked to the driver's side of my dad's pickup, stuck his head through the window where I was sitting and started cussing Bill, using every word in Chris' formidable vocabulary. The "cussing out" must have gone on for a full two minutes, maybe a little more, because Chris had plenty to say about the efficacy of Bill not stealing his apples.

Once finished he glanced at me, and said, "And that goes for you, too." Bill received his full attention for two minutes and I got a nanosecond of "and that goes for you, too." He didn't even swear at me. That in and of itself established a record that will never be broken.

I understand why Bill insisted on being careful.

It turned out that I, in the rush to escape, forgot to turn the key on. No small wonder it didn't start. No wonder we didn't escape. No wonder Bill got cussed out. He was unhappy but not for long.

Katy's Nipple and Harvey's field in the foreground

5. ON BEING FORCED TO SAY "I'M SORRY"AND THANKING GOD FOR HARVEY NEBEL

Every Spring Dad trailed his cows from Kane to Dryhead Creek. The actual "sit in the saddle, breathe dust, suffer snow, rain, and boredom" fell to me. It always did. Bill, and sometimes, Cowboy Bob would come along once in a while. It was while punching cows, pushing them up on the mountain, that I realized that Bob was part John Wayne and, maybe even related to him. When Cowboy Bob went with us, he'd sit tall in the saddle, never slouching. He sat, his Stetson always just so, a silk bandana tied tight around his neck, an insulated leather vest buttoned up, wearing a long sleeved, snappy shirt and Levis with Tony Lama boots. He looked plenty impressive. Unless, of course, his horse laid down with him sitting primly in the saddle; then he didn't look nearly so impressive. I was a slouch. I wore Keds tennis shoes, hand me down J.C. Penney denim britches, and short sleeved tees. Sometimes I wore shirts missing buttons, sleeves, and pockets. I never looked cowboy pretty. Bob did. Hence, I called him Cowboy Bob.

Harvey Nebel trailed cows to Dryhead with us once, or maybe we went with him. He brought this real, genuine, hairy buffalo robe to keep himself warm. Intent on suffering only the comforts of home, he drove Ward Meyer's motor home. The buffalo

146

robe was one that the Crow Indians used to get themselves through the winter without freezing to death. Harv was proud of it. I was certainly impressed and stayed impressed until three in the morning when Harv woke everyone up because his buffalo robe wasn't keeping the frost off his butt. It didn't help that he insisted on sleeping off the ground on a thin, canvas-covered cot. He probably would have been warmer if he and that buffalo robe had slept on the ground with the rest of the migrant labor.

Bacon, eggs, and pork-grease grit do not taste good at three in the morning. Nothing does. In fact, they do not taste at all. Especially with Dad laughing at Sexy-Rex and myself for not wanting to be awake and at Harvey for freezing his butt under the weight of his super-duper buffalo robe.

Eventually it was clear that there was more to Dad and Harv than I had any reason to know. It took forever for me to discover what. The last thing I remember of their relationship was two very old men sitting in a hospital room at the North Big Horn Hospital, Dad holding Harv's hand, with Harv dying and nobody saying a word. I learned later that nothing needed to be said, that it had already been said and that I, and Sexy Rex, and everybody else were just footnotes on their way to somewhere else.

It was on the Dryhead trail that I learned that Harv had been a fair cow hand: that he'd even taken the salt out of the rough string a time or two: that like everyone else he'd been thrown: that once he lit the ground, straddled a barbed wire fence and his mother had to hold his private parts together while getting him to a doctor: that he wasn't always a yellow school bus driver who liked throwing me off the bus.

It was later I realized there was a conspiracy, a plan in place that originated with my Dad and Harv. It was a plot that originated before I could think. In retrospect I imagine Harvey talking to my old man. Undoubtedly Dad was all decked out in his denim bib overalls. I imagine that it took place on the road below the house between the Frank Good homestead and the spot where little Joe Brocious owned an old log cabin and a hayfield. Harv waved Dad down and both sat in their respective trucks, the engines off, talking about nothing at all and whether Porcupine creek would be worth fishing that year. Dad said, "Harv, if that little shit gets out of line, throw his ass off the bus." And Harv said, "I'll do it, Newel." And Harv did. The practice was this: if I got out of line on the bus, out I'd go. No hard feelings. See you tomorrow.

Once Harv caught me swearing. Harv heard me. I said "son of a bitch." I said it to no one in particular, but I said it out loud. The next morning my sister and I were down at the end of the road to catch the school bus and Harv wouldn't let me on. I was standing flat footed on the ground looking up at Sexy Rex standing on the top step of the bus. Harv was prepared to have Sexy Rex beat the hell out of me for insulting Harv's honor and that of Sexy Rex's mother and everyone else that Harvey had ever known since the beginning of time. The price for me being allowed on the bus on that cold brisk November day was saying, "I'm sorry."

This was a pivotal moment in my otherwise non-stellar, flat-lined existence. If I didn't get on the bus, Dad was going to beat my butt raw. No question. Probably more than once. If I didn't get on the bus I would have to walk twelve miles to school and that wasn't going to happen. No question. Mother wasn't going to drive me. No question about that, either. In that moment I thought of hitting Sexy Rex in the balls. He was standing right above me; they were right there for the pounding. I had the opportunity. But the truth was also written right there on the side of the bus in pure English. If, I, by some stretch of my imagination, "won," I'd lose. Harv would never let me on the bus. Especially if I won. I was dead. I had no choice.

There I was standing on the ground, Sexy Rex towering three feet over me and Harvey sitting in the cat-bird driver's seat, his hand on the door handle and an amused expression on his face. It was an event that I could not have planned for or anticipated. In that brief instant of time I saw myself sitting under a leafless cottonwood with nowhere to go and no options. I had this mental picture flash through my mind of me trudging twelve miles in a snow storm. It wasn't a pleasant thought. I was left with "sorry."

Those thoughts and that conclusion took six seconds of my life. The conclusion however was monumental, extending way beyond an embarrassed, cussing, cursing, snot-nosed, nondescript, kid. It affected the lives of unsuspecting people, people who never heard of Harvey Nebel, people who had they known, would have begged Harvey to allow me on the bus without any of the fuss.

Thirty years later I was standing alone at counsel table in the Los Angeles Superior Court representing the plaintiff. Across from me, representing the defendants, were six of the finest LA attorneys that six hundred fifty dollars and an hour could buy. Before the case was called I glanced at those five men and one woman. I thought of Harvey and Sexy Rex and had to smile. At that moment in time I thanked God for Harvey Nebel.

It isn't easy to explain but I was ready. I had been preparing for that moment in time since the very day I tried to get on the bus and Harv said, "Hold on. Not so fast." I was no longer the eleven - year-old boy standing flat footed looking at Sexy Rex's belly button, mentally examining the definition of "winning" as fast as my enfeebled mind would allow. On that later morning in downtown L.A. before Harv's proverbial "bus" had left his proverbial garage I had examined in detail every eventuality, every possible argument that could be made, every course of action. No one was going to force me to say I was sorry as the price of getting on the bus. I made sure I was already on the bus, that I was driving. All because of Harvey Nebel.

So God bless him and God bless Sexy Rex. They made me a lot of money and I have enjoyed spending every dime. I am not saying that I won every time I stepped before the bench to argue a case. I surely didn't. Harvey Nebel, however, made all the difference. He put me on Bobby Frost's road less traveled by.

6. MASTERING THE FINE ART OF FISHING AND HIDING BEHIND CEDAR POSTS

During one of those spring "trail the cows to Dryhead creek campouts," Bill and I stopped above the Tillet Fish Hatchery. I say above because folks had built a barbed wire corral around a spring north of where the fish hatchery sits, and for generations dating back to 1882, cow men had stopped there. It was meant to service the trail herds that every spring walked the rocky road to the Pryor Mountain pastures. Every year we stopped there just as they had.

In the late 1950s, sitting in the afternoon shade of a juniper tree, cows standing in the wire corral, waiting for Dad to bring the yellow grub box, Bill and I realized that we not just hungry, we were bordering on starving.

In the midst of this belly anguish, we realized we were six hundred yards from a fish hatchery. It's a rhetorical question, but what better place to fish than a fish hatchery? Fishing was a little difficult with no line, no hooks, no bait, and nothing but ingenuity, but we were determined. Below the hatchery, the water ran into a manmade lake. We drove several huge trout into small tributaries and literally jumped on them, catching them with our bare hands and whacking them on the head. Then we snuck through the juniper trees and sagebrush to our camp. Once there, we'd roast, toast, and eat them. Trout tasted good because we were hungry. They tasted even better once we remembered to bring salt, pepper, and a frying pan.

In recorded history, we were never caught fishing at the fish hatchery, never caught eating fish hatchery fish either. Once, we were chased by a pickup truck; fortunately we were on horseback. After we saw the pickup bouncing along on a dirt road, we ran our horses, hanging onto their backs like we were guilty of something. Turned out, we were chased by Jay Kelsey and whoever was driving. I doubt if they would have even bothered to chase us, but we were galloping across the sage brush flat south of the hatchery and they must have equated running with obvious guilt.

In our minds, we were caught dead to rights because we had been fishing without licenses at a protected fish hatchery, a place where nobody could fish even if they had licenses. But Jay Kelsey didn't know that. The pickup reached the wire gate a long time before we did and was up the hill behind it before we reached it. By the time we arrived, the gate post had grown substantially. As we approached, there was Jay Kelsey hiding on both sides of the gate post, trying to make himself invisible. How does a two hundred ten pound man do that?

When we were within ten feet, Kelsey jumped out of hiding--as though we couldn't see him--and grabbed Bill's horse by the bridle. He commenced to tell him everything he could conjure up and nothing at all about our fishing adventures. (The normal lecture.)

Footnote in passing: At lecturing, Jay Kelsey couldn't hold a candle to Chris Schatz. If Chris just started talking, merely opening his mouth, he could peel sun-dried paint right off a tall wall. Kelsey, by comparison, should he get up real early in the morning, couldn't even raise a bubble. That's not to say he didn't try. About a minute into the lecture, Jay Kelsey let go of the bridle to Bill's horse and looked sternly at me. I smiled as I nudged the bay through the wire gate.

Jay said to me, "Who the hell do you think you are, you little shit head?" I didn't reply. At the time I had no idea who I was. I was, however, secure in one fact that Jay had missed: There was nothing he could do to Bill and me for running our horses across BLM land. What was incredibly funny was Jay Kelsey hiding his considerable self behind a skinny cedar post. I remember thinking, do adults actually do that?

Indeed, they did.

7. STOP THE BUS?

Harvey Nebel did have it in for us. And we for him. One school evening Bill and I were watching the water flow under the Shoshone Bridge, checking on the fish hooks we hid there for that off day when we would actually go fishing. We never did. They are probably still where we left them: That'd be under the flat green rock on the left side of the south entrance to the bridge; they'd be in the tin with the picture of fish hooks on the top side, along with a spool of fish line. That's where they'd be.

In the process of taking inventory we found the maggot ridden carcass of a very dead ewe. Its former owner had dropped it off, having no further use for the old girl. Guessing from the rate of deterioration that would be have been about two weeks earlier. Most people would have looked at that smelly, bloated, hunk of wool draped over ribs and backbone, took a deep breath, and gotten out of there. The smell alone would drive a normal person away, strongly resolving not to come back, not to get out of the truck, and to move right on by. Not Bill and me. We saw a prime opportunity to cause Harvey to stop the bus.

The Shoshone river bridge was actually meant to convey trains across a river somewhere. In the early 1900s it had been hauled in from some distant place like Virginia or Deer Creek, Arkansas and set up as a conveyance across the Shoshone, connecting one side with the other. The timbers were tall and thick. The old bridge itself was long, lean and black from engine smoke and age. We found some rope that some one had thrown in the trash and that had ended up at the South entrance to the bridge.

Bill climbed on top of the bridge some twenty five feet about the ground and pulled the rope through the utmost upright, a steel structural rod that held the two sides of the bridge together. We secured one end of the rope around the ewe's neck and foreleg and pulled the old girl up until she was level with what tomorrow morning would be Harvey's school bus windshield. And there she hung dead center in the middle of the bridge entrance, turning slowly in the evening breeze, white, roly poly maggots dropping onto the road surface like popcorn from a skillet. Five feet on either side was river and bridge. Harvey would have to stop. There was no going around without popping that bloated carcass.

I was excited. Stop Harvey was the idea. Cause a commotion. Everyone would tell someone else and Harvey would be delayed minutes from his appointed route. He picked us up at 7:14 a.m., made a stop for the Giffords from Crystal Creek at the railroad crossing on 14A, then he turned down the county road to the Shoshone bridge. After he crossed the river, he'd pick up the Scheelers, the Schatz, the Tillys, the Bassets and the Schneiders. But before he did, before he got that far, he had to cross the bridge.

And there it was, no longer twisting but hanging just where we'd left it. Harvey stopped. Sexy Rex climbed up on the yellow hood just in front of the flashing red lights and cut her down with Harv's pocket knife. It didn't take as long as I had hoped but still it gave Harvey something to talk about.

"Those damn kids. What were they thinking? Too much time on their hands."

Then he glanced at me through the rear view mirror. I smiled and shook my head no. My body language said "no" but most important, he didn't believe me. Except for telling Bill, I never said a word. Bottom line: We were late in getting to Bill's bus stop, late getting to Pete, late in getting to Joyce Gams, late in getting to school and just plain late. No one seemed to mind.

That dead piece of mutton was not so dead after all. It stopped the bus.

8. LUNCH WITH HARRY

Located in the center of the town of Kane were the remnants of the Neeley Hotel, once owned by the now deceased Harry Quarnstrom. It sat empty and unused, its exterior abused by wind, rain, snow and the heat of the sun, yet inviting to a couple of punk kids like Bill and me. It was difficult to get inside without being seen. The watchful Mrs. Ellis was at the post office a hundred yards to the north, Mrs. Nebel a quarter of a mile up the hill, and the section boss' wife keeping house a hundred yards due east. It was next to impossible, and always a challenge to do so without being caught. To our credit, we were never caught.

Harry died and no one moved a thing from that place; it was a treasure trove--the most interesting place in the diminishing town. The front door faced south and was always locked. Inside were display cases where once Harry sold candy bars, loaves of bread, cans of peanut butter, and potato strings. I know about the candy bars because I purchased the one and only *Idaho Spud* I've ever had from him with a dime my mother gave me. It wasn't much.

At the time of Bill and me, I do not know how long Harry had been dead. The place was dusty; so it had been a while. Directly in the middle of the room was a large pot-bellied stove and an empty wood box. Bill and I never built a fire in it. There

158

were multiple chairs sitting haphazardly around the stove. To the left was a huge rolltop desk with dozens of compartments above the drawers, and a whole lot of drawers.

Behind the desk was a large, steel safe with an eight inch thick metal door that could have stored the crown jewels and probably did. It was always open and the jewels weren't there anymore. It was an unresolved mystery as to what Harry could have possibly kept in that safe. It had half a dozen lockable metal inserts, like safety deposit boxes. We hauled those up on top of the hills behind Kane and buried them in the bentonite-crusted dirt, thus keeping all of our invaluable valuables from being discovered. They are still there and still invaluable. Bill and I never went back. The key: Four flat rocks due west of the large flat rock that sat in the middle of the third draw. In other words, I don't know where those metal boxes are buried. The shovel, however, is still in the draw, if someone wants to look.

Upstairs, a hall went through the middle of the building. On each side one room after another was furnished with unmade beds, chests of drawers, wash basins, broken mirrors, mattresses, and bedding--all covered in dust and rat droppings. In the back of the building were shelves, floor-to-ceiling, storing everything known to man. We had no idea what all that stuff was, but there was certainly a collection.

The back door locked from the inside. We got inside through a loose board that didn't look loose. Once inside, we would unlock the back door and have free ingress, egress. We were always careful to lock it when we left. The last one crawling through and under the one by twelve that covered the hole in the back wall locked the door.

Through the back door and sitting a couple of yards to the left was an above ground root cellar. It had a locked Master Lock on it. The latch itself covered the phillips wood screws so that nobody could get in by removing the screws. It warranted investigation. Bill and I gently pulled the entire latch off the door frame, thus allowing the door to open. To keep everyone else out, we put the latch screws back into the holes in the door frame, and pushed the latch flush. It looked locked.

The root cellar had a high, rounded dirt roof. Inside was floor-to-ceiling shelving on three sides. The interior was about ten feet long and six feet wide. To the unobservant, there was absolutely nothing inside on the shelving except one old mason jar without a lid, very little dust, a few woodscrews, and an empty beer bottle missing its label.

Behind the door, however, Mrs. Quarnstrom had left row upon row of canned peaches in quart jars: four complete shelves of them. She'd canned them in Mason jars, cutting the peaches in half, leaving the skin on, and the peaches bathed in thick syrup. If there was a contest for canning peach halves in Mason jars, Mrs. Quarnstrom would take all of the prizes, win all of the ribbons, and be number one and first in her class. In fact, she'd be first in every class. They were that good, that memorable.

Bill and I would take a bottle of peaches from the root cellar into the hotel, making sure the coast was double clear--that Mrs. Nebel wasn't driving by on her way to the post office, that the section house folks weren't home, or if they were, the Mrs. was washing dishes, dusting, or doing what section house moms do, and not looking out the window at the hotel, and that Scary Larry's mom was inside and not standing in her yard talking with a postal patron or yelling at Larry for not feeding the pigs the way she wanted them fed.

Inside the hotel and market, we'd sit in the chairs that surrounded the pot-bellied stove and kept it captive. In the quiet of the deserted building, safe as we'd ever be in our future lives, we'd comfortably pass the bottle of peaches to each other, spearing peach halves with our pocket knives, and eating dinner. It was only one course, but that course was fantastic.

Thank you, Harry Q.

Neeley Hotel purchased by Harry Quarnstrom

9. EPILOGUE

Several weeks ago I saw Bill. He was hunting birds with several of his stepsons. He stopped and I told him to hunt wherever he damn well pleased. In passing he mentioned that we should get together and talk over old times.

I smiled and said, "The older we get the better we were!"

He looked at me and said, "What?"

What indeed!

Yesterday I was at the post office in that thriving metropolis of Lovell, Wyoming. After being introduced to an elderly woman she looked at me and asked who I was. I told her I was raised in Kane and that no one knew me. She said "I know someone who lived there. His name is Bill. Bill? You know him? He was raised in Kane."

I said, "I did."

She stared at me for what seemed a long time and said, "He lives in a very strange world."

Strange indeed!

There are a hundred stories to tell but I am going to quit here. Sometime in the future Bill and I will get together. We'll remember those six cent Mississippi Crook Cigars we bought at the pool hall in Lovell from a fellow named Mortenson. I was ten. Bill was eleven. We'll remember the hot ashes falling on the horse's shoulders, the horse turning inside out and going every which way but loose.

163

We'll talk about Pete stealing Officer Meek's cop car, driving it into the outback and the fool forgetting where he parked it. We'll remember being out in the black of night to steal some fresh pie cherries from Mr. and Mrs. Brown's cherry tree, of Bill peering over the front gate to make sure the coast was clear and putting his hand down on someone's warm muscular arm. I'll remind him that he lit out, passing me in an eye blink, like he was called from the other side and really didn't want to go.

We'll remember that strange, incredible world of our youth when mother thought Bill was perfect and I could do no wrong. We'll remind each other, laugh at our craziness, because we'll know. It happened just that way.

CHAPTER 13

CONVERSATIONS OVER SUPPER

No one comes from nowhere. Everyone comes from somewhere. Like it or not, everyone receives at birth a sack of river rocks to carry around. Sometimes they're big ones, emotional scars, open wounds carried and nursed by their parents since time began. A man or a woman can spend a lifetime trying to drop those rocks and rid themselves of the emotional scars and wounds their parents saddled them with. And they're heavy rocks not so easily falling out of a sack. Most never succeed. It's just too hard. Some of us never try.

My father's people were like that, a bunch of ragamuffin misfits that arrived in the Basin in a boxcar pulled by a smoke belching steam engine, stopping at the rail head, which for those few days was located in Frannie, Wyoming: Frannie, the biggest little town in the state. The eldest, Estella, was born in 1884. She was twelve. The year of their arrival was 1896--the year Kane, Wyoming graduated from being called Riley Kane's place to just plain "Kane." She arrived with her brothers and sisters, getting off a boxcar in the high desert, amid stacks of new creosote soaked railroad ties, rows of steel rails, boxes of steel spikes, steel plates, and teams of horses pulling slip-scrapers, dragging road graders and steel rimmed freight wagons.

Estella's siblings were born two years apart and never in the same place. Their birth places read like a Rand McNally listing of places not to visit: Farmington, Utah: Wilford, Idaho: Castle, Montana: Wilford, Idaho again: Great Falls, Montana: and lastly, Farmington, Utah. Forest Eugene was ten. William Louis was eight. Jesse Fountain was six. Martha Pearl was four, and Rose was two. There were no adults: no mom to help them figure out what to do. No one to hug them, make them some pancakes or boil a pot of grits. That mother had died giving birth to Rose in Farmington, Utah. There was no Dad. Where he was, was unknown. He showed up later. In family lore no one seemed to think his absence abnormal. Perhaps it wasn't. Today he'd be jailed for child endangerment, abandonment.

Estella, all twelve years of her, was in charge. She asked a Crow Indian, a passerby working for the Chicago, Burlington and Quincy railroad, where Lovell was located. Why she wanted to go there was anybody's guess to which only God knows the answer. Looking across that windswept plain of salt sage and grease wood at the West Pryor Mountain could not have been encouraging. They were hungry, starving, thirsty, and alone.

From Frannie this group of kids with a two year old baby walked to Lovell, a distance of fifteen miles. The twelve year old carried the infant, Rose. Forest Eugene held Jess's hand to keep the four year old from falling behind. All they owned is what they wore. The next two years they lived in a tent at the end of Nevada Avenue on the Shoshone River. When *it was cold those chldren were cold. When it was hot, they were hot. Rose was four when they moved to Himes, changing one river bottom for another.*

The Himes locale is on the north end of the canyon, where the Big Horn River flows through Sheep Mountain. Literally, on the river's edge they lived in a small two room frame schoolhouse. that Jess, Lou, Forest and their father, Joseph Henry, had moved from a neighboring school section to about twenty-feet from the edge of the river.

In 1965 the U.S. Government, under their "we can do anything we want" divine authority protocol, burned the shack down to the ground. They did this to prevent Rose from accomplishing her promised threat to move back into it. As if she would! As if she could! In burning the worthless, weather beaten, windowless shack, the government drove their sixty thousand dollar pickup trucks onto private property with a can of diesel fuel and a box of blue tipped matches. At the time Rose and her husband Lee Hoffman were being forced to vacate their farm on the Iona side of the Shoshone River to allow for the filling of the Reservoir. The rancor between the different sides was high and intense.

In those days folks visited, folks talked. There was nothing else to do. There were no radios, no TVs, nothing to occupy each other's attention except eating and conversation.

Most of their early conversations occurred whilst sitting together eating supper at a pine plank table in the two room school house in Himes, Wyoming, a mere spot, a small dot listed on maps under the categories entitled "used to be" and "never was." The first noted conversation, however, was at the Clarke ranch house situated up against the Big Horn Mountain. Later it was known as Moncur Springs, so named after Estella Howe Moncur and her husband Will. They owned it.

CONVERSATIONS - 1

"Pass the biscuits. . . and the butter," Jess said, hesitating. "Please."

"You better say please or you'll be starvin'," Estella said. She glanced about the table. "Butter? Where's the butter? Rose, I think it's in the ice box. Would you get it?"

Rose laughed. "The ice box with no ice? That ice box?"

A chair creaked. Its legs scraped the rough pine wood floor as it was pushed away from the table.

Estella surveyed the table. She said, "Forest, you're lookin' peaked. You get enough? Your plate's empty."

"Just getting started, Stel. Ain't ate all day, not since this mornin' early. I'm feelin' I could eat a Belgian stud horse and chase its skinny rider. Trouble is my stomach is shrunk up so I gotta take it easy. It's a dirty trick played on starvin' men."

There was momentary silence, punctuated by the sound of forks scraping porcelain plates, knives

168

sawing at fresh venison steak, a glass being set down, water being poured into a glass. Someone coughed. No one said anything.

Rose sat down, handing Jess a square bowl containing homemade butter and a butter knife.

Forest commented to no one in particular. "Saw them buzzards yesterday up on the Pryor. Right where Lou said they'd be. Above the north rim. Lots of them. Must be couple thousand dead sheep up there; that many birds. So many. Like to darken the sky."

"Near three," Jess said. "Maybe more. Damn things."

"Three thousand. Didn't know there were that many! Reckon that'll solve the sheep problem," Forest said as he glanced at Jess between mouthfuls of skillet fried potatoes.

"Dead sheep don't eat grass," Jess said matter of factly. "Not on the north rim anyways."

"Not anywhere," Lou enjoined. "I don't think this is over. I don't. I think it's just beginning."

Forest glanced at Lou, "Lots of birds, can't count them." he said. "Not just buzzards. Crows, too. Ravens, magpies. Saw some hawks. There were more magpies than I'd want to count. I ain't never seen so many. It was like there was some sorta magpie gatherin'."

Rose dished herself some potatoes from the skillet. Finished, she set the skillet down, glancing at her brother. She said, "Lou, what do you suppose happened?"

"Can't say."

"Best not to talk about it," Jess replied. "Less said the better."

"Thought you and Lou were up that way."

"We was," Jess replied.

Silence. Then a muffled bang and Ring barking.

Forest looked up. "What was that? Did you hear that?" he asked.

Forest and Lou stood up, stepped outside. Jess followed, walking around the table, pulling his hat down on his head. They were gone for the better part of five minutes. A few minutes later the three men came back inside.

"What was it?" Rose asked Jess.

"Damned if I know," Jess replied.

"Some bird walkin' on the roof. Maybe a squirrel," Lou said.

Forest responded, shaking his head, "No. Too loud for a bird or a squirrel."

"Well, I don't know. Nothin' out there that I can see," Jess said.

Rose looked at him. "Maybe," she said, "it's the ghosts of them sheep you killed. Why'd you have to do that anyway? Three thousand."

"It's either them or us. Sheep ruin the grass. Kill it. Leave nothin' for a cow. Pound a water hole 'til its turned into a mud hole; water not drinkable. Nothin' can use it. Remember the grass between Lovell and Greybull? There was lots of grass, sage to a horse's belly. Look at it now. Bare as a goat's ass. That's them damn sheep. They kill it for everybody."

"Well? What happened exactly?" Forest asked. "Up there on the mountain?"

"Stupid question, Far. We know what happened," Rose said. "Real clear. Now that we hate sheep so much, what are you going to do with Red's ewe, the one that Snyder fellow gave him last year? Every morning she's standin' out there bleatin'; especially when he's slow to feed her."

"Well, Rose, we could take her up on the East Pryor and throw her off the mountain."

"You better not."

Lou smiled. "We should eat it. Nothin' like lamb chops."

"Nothin' that won't gag a maggot," Jess replied. "Mutton leaves an awful taste in the mouth."

Estella laughed. "Not if you cook it right," she said. "Ya gotta cook it right."

"Well, Stell, case you ain't learned it, there ain't no way to cook sheep right."

"Yeah, yeah but come December you'll be wearin' sheepskin."

"They are good for a coat. I gotta say that for them."

"Eatin' that ewe be like eatin' a pet rat or Ol' Ring, thet dog. You imagine cookin' Ring, servin' him for dinner?"

"I'll bet old Ring would be tasty compared to that damn ewe."

Jess glanced at Forest chewing on a buttered biscuit, honey dripping on his fingers. Taking his time he licked the honey from his forefinger then the palm of his hand, taking another bite before he spoke.

"Well, Far," Jess said, answering his question. " Lou and I was up on the north rim of the East Pryor. We'd ridden past the ice caves a couple of miles. It was dark but the moon was up. We could see pretty good." Jess paused."Pass the tators and that gravy. Stell, that's good gravy. You outdid yourself, girl. And them biscuits! I could use another."

Rose passed the plate to him. Jess took the plate, selected a biscuit and proceeded to slather it with butter.

"Jeez, Jess," Rose said, "I want to know how a skinny light weight like you can eat so much."

"It's my hollow leg," Jess answered.

"Thanks, Sis," Jess said to Rose. "Anyways," Jess continued, "so we was ridin' up past the ice caves a mile or two, fixin' to drop down off the mountain onto Sage Creek. Come across a herd of sheep. A big herd. Didn't see the sheepherder. There was some dogs barking. Sounded far off. Somethin' had them stirred up. Sheep was a millin'. Thought maybe a cat, maybe coyotes had them stirred up. I don't know what. Hard to tell frankly--it was dark."

"Probably a cat!" Lou said. "They was runnin' in bunches, like they do when dogs are chasin' them. Rose, you hoggin' those potatoes and those biscuits? I need a biscuit to mop up this gravy." Lou smiled. "Trouble was, Far, they was right up against that east rim and runnin' and

172

dodgin' in bunches. It was pretty quiet except for those sheep."

Jess glanced at Red. "Boy, did you take care of those saddle horses?"

"Yes, sir. I did," the boy answered.

"Rub them down?"

"Yes, sir. Far as I could. And grained them. Put them in the horse pasture like you said. Uncle Jess, that one grey–he's looking a little lame. His foot is bleeding."

Jess looked at the boy. "Bleeding? That's not good. Pass that water pitcher would you, Rose? Lame, you say. The grey? We'll have a look after supper. You and me. Think he stepped on somethin'? He bleedin' bad?"

"Yes, sir. Probably. It ain't bad though. Just a little."

"Well?" The voice was feminine and impatient. Estella was looking at Jess.

Jess smiled. "Tell me, Red," he said, "you want to eat that ewe of yours? What do you call it? Does she have a name?"

"No, Uncle Jess, just Sheep. That's all."

"Sheep? That's a hell of a name."

"Jess, finish your story."

"I'm gettin' to it, Pearl. Don't wanna rush. Might choke on Stell's biscuits." Jess took another bite. "So anyways, what Lou is sayin' is that a couple of sheep was real close to the edge on the east rim. One fell over. That part was sorta accidental. The next just jumped after it. One after another."

173

Rose laughed. "Sure. And you were just watching her."

"No. No. Rose," Jess replied. "It was accidental. I saw that one backed up against the ledge then bein' pushed by the others tryin' to get away from Lou and me. Over she went. I think they was scared of our saddle horses. That's what I think. We didn't have any dogs. It bein' dark, they was just tryin' to get away from us. One fell. She was backin' up, lost her footing then fell over the side. Just disappeared. One was followed by another. Suddenly they started jumpin' into the dark, disappearin'. It was one after another 'til there weren't any left. We ain't talkin' long, neither. That first one fell, then another and then they was all jumpin'. Fact is, after that first one they was runnin' and jumpin' over the edge. It was crazy. So we just got out of the way. Didn't want to discourage any of them."

"Did it kill them?" Red asked.

"Well, boy, they hit the bottom. Bounced once and laid real still. That was about it. Say, you worried about your Uncle Lou takin' Ol' Sheep up there on the mountain and throwin' her off? I'd start worryin' if I was you."

Red shook his head 'no' chewing on what was left of buttered biscuit.

Forest laughed. "I'll bet it was mighty disturbin' seein' all those sheep committin' suicide right in front of you."

"Not so much," Jess said.

Jess picked up another baking powder biscuit and said to no one in particular, "Lou and I had some

174

trouble yesterday on Dryhead Creek. I ain't told you 'bout it. Came across a couple of riders. I think they ride for that outfit that lost those sheep a week or so ago."

The table was silent except for the pouring of water in a tin cup and the sound of forks on plates.

"Who might they be?" Estella poured gravy on her venison steak, then glanced at Jess for the answer to her question.

"Don't know. Saw them over on the other end of West Pryor six, eight months ago. It was at Warren. They was havin' a good time. You know the place?"

"The other side of Frannie," Rose offered. "What were you doin' over there?"

"This was last fall when I seen them. I was looking for a bull that I had missin'."

"What were they doin'?"

"Drinkin'. Socializin' with them girls. Seemed to be in a good mood."

"So, what happened?" Estella paused, looking at Jess. " You weren't visitin' no girls were you?"

"No, I weren't visitin' no girls six months ago. We was on Dry Head Creek yesterday."

"I meant anytime."

"No, I weren't visitin' no girls yesterday, neither. Anyway, one of these fellows had a scar above his eye. Fancied himself a boxer. Looked mean enough. He got to talkin' to Lou here. Real aggressive."

Lou laughed. "Rose, got any more of those roastin' ears? This story is about to get unbelievable."

Rose passed him the plate full of corn. She said, "Better save some room for apple pie, Lou. I worked on it all afternoon."

"Don't worry, Rose, I'll have room."

Pearl was watching Estella. She said, "Better sit down and eat, Stell. You can't be gettin' no skinnier. You'll turn sideways and disappear." She turned her attention back to her younger brother. "So, Jess, what happened?" Pearl asked.

Jess swallowed the biscuit and drank some water. "Well," he said, "that fellow I was tellin' you about, he got to givin' Lou here a terrible time. So Lou offers to set him straight. That fellow accepts and he's off his horse before he could get a proper invite, all ready to make a little war. Anyways, Lou and this fellow gets to it. Lou took his time blockin' punches with his nose, gettin' himself beat on. I gotta admire him; he was wantin' it to be a fair fight so he lets this fellow get in a few swings to encourage him."

Lou shook his head. He said, "That ain't so. Don't believe a word. I won that fight straight up and I didn't block any punches with my nose. Besides Jess didn't get off his horse. He was just watchin' like he had nothin' to do."

"True enough. Except this other fellow sees his friend gettin' whooped and decides to jump in and pull his pard's bacon out of the fire. Right then I was forced to lend a hand."

176

"Lend a hand?"

"I pulled my forty-five and invited him to stay in the saddle."

"No kiddin'? You didn't?" Rose asked, suddenly interested. "What did he do?"

"Well, girl, he considered his options right careful. Then he stayed in the saddle."

Lou laughed. "Okay. Jess did keep that other fellow in the saddle but I did all the whoopin' up on this fellow. Trouble was he didn't want to stay whooped. Had to explain it to him. But we ironed it out. Settled our differences."

Martha smiled. "I'll bet. You're goin' to say you all parted friends after you all had a group hug."

"I wouldn't go quite that far. T'weren't no huggin'. There any more of those tators, Rose? What about some peas?"

Rose replied, "There's some potatoes and a spoonful of peas left."

"Pass them here, would you? Any of that venison steak? I'm feeling a bit thin with all this talk."

"Why in the first place did he want to fight like that, Lou? You two insult him?"

"Seems they was feelin' poorly losin' all those sheep. Thought we had somethin' to do with it."

"What did you say to him, Jess? What got them all stirred up?"

"I didn't say nothin' except 'keep your seat'. Lou did all the explainin'. Told that boy he had it all wrong. I swear Lou had him on his back three times

177

before he became a believer. He did that John L. Sullivan tap dance on his nose."

Red giggled.

Lou turned to look at him. "What are you laughin' at, Red?"

"You dancin' on his nose. It ain't big enough, Uncle Lou."

"Maybe he had a big nose boy. Did you ever think of that?"

Rose Howe at 15 years of age

CONVERSATIONS - 2

Telephones and party lines came to the Kane flat and to the folks who lived there. Some got them. Some didn't. Martha Pearl Good was among those who didn't. She lived in the Frank Good farmstead with her offspring Newel (Red), Lillian, Virgil, Joe, and Naomi, as well as her husband, Frank. The old log house was located a quarter of a mile south of where the causeway crosses the reservoir on Highway 14A and a couple hundred yards east of the railroad tracks.

The only present evidence of the log cabin is a block of cement poured by Newel Howe in 1953 on the east end of the structure as a porch of sorts. Out front and east of the kitchen were three large lilac bushes that turned a violent purple each spring.

Forest stood in the doorway. Behind him his bay horse stood at the rail, reins wrapped loosely around the pole.

"Far," Pearl exclaimed. "Come right in. How nice to see you. We were just fixin' to eat a little supper. It's not much. Want to sit down and eat with us? We'd sure like it if you would."

"Thanks, Pearl. Don't mind if I do. Gettin' a little saddle worn, thin at the edges."

"It's not much. Corn on the cob. Fresh bread and some green beans."

"Just what I was wantin', Pearl."

"And some boiled crooknecks, too. Got some crooknecks."

"The bread smells good."

"Move over, Joey. Virgil, get Uncle Far a chair."

"Where you been, Uncle Far?" Lillian asked. "You feelin' good?"

"Better, Lil. Been up at the Clarke Place. Building Stell some barns. Got Jess' cows pushed up on the mountain. Thought I'd take Red up there with me when I go back. How about you, girl?"

"I'm fine, Uncle Far, but I ain't been shot."

"Good for you, girl. Bein' shot ain't what it's cracked up to be. You don't mind, do you, Pearl? Me takin' Red up on the mountain?"

"No. Not at all. No doubt he wants to get outta here."

Lillian said, "Did it hurt, Uncle Far? Gettin' shot? Did it hurt real bad?"

"Lillian, Uncle Forest don't want to talk about gettin' shot."

Forest smiled at the girl. "Well, Lil, it didn't feel like smokin' a Sunday rum-soaked, Cuban cigar and takin' a bath in a hot tub. I don't recommend it. Let me say that."

"Does it hurt? I mean still?"

"Only when it rains. It starts to rain and it starts actin' up somethin' fierce."

"Jess said he could use Red pushin' them cows the rest the way on top. Say, I got a question been botherin' me. Last week, when I was through here, I saw all them folks up there on the hill behind

181

Kane. Top of Katy's Nipple, too. Musta' been forty or fifty. What was that all about? They were all wavin'. So I waved back. Some kind of party?"

"You mean last Monday?"

"Yeah, last Monday." Forest paused, seeing a child come into the kitchen. "I see you got a stray runnin' around loose, Martha." He smiled at the little girl. Where's Lou?"

"I do. Lou and Lida were goin' to Lovell. Left her here. Elsie, show Uncle Far how old you are."

The little girl help up three fingers.

"Three? And you can count already."

She nodded her head.

"But you can't talk? Is that it?"

She shook her head no.

Forest laughed.

"Those people on the hill," Red said, "that was funny, Uncle Far."

"It was funny," his mother, Pearl, said. "You know, Far, everybody gots phones. Exceptin' us. We don't. Some smart turd called from Lovell. Said that dam above Cody broke, that flood water was comin' fast. Said that it'd be here soon and that we should head for higher ground. Everybody but us knew about it. All them folks in Kane ran to the hill waitin' for the flood. Here we were just as happy as hogs in a slop pail knowin' nothin'. There they were coolin' in the breeze. I was puttin' up twenty quarts of corn in that heat. I could have used the break."

Forest laughed. "You down here puttin' up corn and a hundred people just watchin' you from

182

the hill. You'd a thought someone would've run down here and warned ya. They were wavin' at me."

"Yeah, you'd have thought. We were happy ignorant. That's what we were. No one even thought we might like to know. 'Fraid they'd get real wet. It was two days later when I went to the post office that I found out we could have drowned. 'Course the real story was there weren't no dam break. Just some turd laughin' hisself silly."

"Newel, grab that cat and throw him out. The rest of you help set the table. Uncle Far is starvin'."

Newel threw the dirty white, long-haired cat out the front door. Ring promptly took it up a tree.

"That damn dog," Pearl said. "He's always givin' that cat fits."

Forest laughed, "Yeah," he said, "but he is careful not to catch him."

Elsie had worked herself close and was leaning on Forest's knee.

Pearl smiled at her. "You should have been here yesterday, Far," Pearl said. "That girl--she was nearly the death of me. It's some story. Lillian, Elsie, and me were walking home from goin' to the post office and the store. We were walkin' down the tracks cause it was shorter, you know. Elsie, she was way out in front sittin' on a rail waitin' for me to catch up. The little knot head busied herself throwin' rocks at the dog. Of a sudden Lil starts screamin' top of her lungs, " Mom, mom there's a train!"

"God, there it was, Far. Comin' right down the track. You know how fast they come."

"I was loud, Uncle Far," Lillian said. "Real loud."

"Sure enough here comes a freight. And they weren't slowin' down. I started runnin'. I mean I was runnin', dropped the bread, busted up the eggs; left the flour all over the tracks. I just threw it down and took off."

Lillian nodded. She said, "All the eggs were busted, Uncle Far."

"Here I was, Far, running for all I was worth. My God, that engineer was layin' on the horn and that child was just sittin' on the track pretty as she could be watchin' me runnin'."

"And Momma was screaming, Uncle Far. And Elsie was just sittin' there watchin' her yellin' at her."

"I wasn't gonna make it, Far. I just wasn't gonna make it. You're not gonna believe this. I don't believe it. Ring was just sittin' there with Elsie throwin' rocks at him and that damn dog beats me to that child and drags her off the tracks by her arm. There he was pullin' her off the rail and down the embankment. Elsie was just a screamin' like she was bein' murdered twice over."

"Elsie was real mad, Uncle Far. Ring wouldn't let go. Look at her arm. Right there."

Pearl ran her hand through Elsie's hair. "You sure scared us didn't you, Elsie."

Elsie smiled at her aunt and nodded.

"Someone was sure lookin' out for us, Far. I swear. I'd never have made it. If it weren't for that dog. Someone somewhere likes that girl. When I reached her I picked that girl up, the train roarin' by and we were just a babblin' like a couple of crazies. It was so close."

"It was God, Uncle Far. He really likes Elsie."

"I'll be damned," Forest said softly. "Well, Lil, lucky He was around ta lend a hand. And that dog, too."

"Yeah, Uncle Far, we ain't yellin' at the dog no more."

"I'll bet he gets to eat first."

Lillian looked at him, thinking. "Naw, Uncle Far, he's gotta eat outside. He ain't got no manners."

"I see," said Forest.

Photo of Shoshone Dam F.J. Hiscock, 1921

CONVERSATIONS - 3

"Jess, did you hear? It's awful." Pearl stared at her younger brother standing in the doorway.

"What?"

"Come in. Sit down. I got this story to tell. Do you want some milk, some bread? Fresh baked? Just pulled it out of the oven."

"That'd be good, Sis. What's got you so upset?"

Jess came inside, pulled a kitchen chair out from the table, and sat down.

"The First State Bank--it burned to the ground. That fellow, what's his name--Herman Dau--the banker, he's gone. Nobody knows where. Before the bank was done burnin', he was gone."

"Gone?"

"He done ran off. It's the talk of the town. Everything is burnt up. The records . . . they are all gone. This fellow, he sure covered his tracks. Some say he had his saddle horse saddled and ready to go before he lit the fire. Others say they saw him get on the train as smoke was a comin' right out of the windows of the bank. Everyone says he lit the fire hisself. This one is some tricky."

"Gone?"

"Jess, stop repeatin' me. Did you hear what I said? I said the bank is burnt plumb to the ground and the banker, he's gone. Folks are really hurt bad. Their money's gone with the banker. Nobody knows nothin'. Folks are hurtin'. Did you hear me? They ain't got no money."

Martha placed a plate in front of him, with two slices of bread, a bowl of yellow butter, and a tall glass of milk. Beads of water were forming on the outside of the glass, running down the sides in little rivulets. Jess looked at the plate then at his sister. He said, "Sis, how much you out?"

"He got me for $45.63 cents. That's all I had but others--they lost everything. I can get by. But other folks--other folks can't. They are hurtin'. They could lose everything. Funny, don't you think? I kept the money in there so I wouldn't lose it. And I lost it."

"Where's the kids? Comin' over here I stopped at the store and bought them some rock candy. Bill Scott threw in some extras. Figured to sweeten them up, he did."

"They're up on the canal wadin'. Coolin' themselves off."

Jess paused, thinking. "Where did he go, Pearl? The banker? What's his name?"

"Herman Dau. You remember him? He bought the bank from that other fellow. Nobody knows where he's gone. The first banker, he's livin' in Lovell now. He ain't got nothin' to do with the Kane bank no more. Lucky him. He got out while the gettin' was good."

"Somebody knows," Jess said, pulling a sack from his shirt pocket, placing it on the table by his plate.

"Are you tryin' to be funny? I talked to the postmaster. I talked to Harry Quarnstrom. I talked to the folks at the section house. Nobody knows. He flew the coop. Took everyone's money. That's what folks say. Rose told me she had no money in that bank. She's never got no money. Spends it quick as she can get it. So she didn't lose any."

"Stell?"

"Nope, nothing. Forest, neither. Lou keeps his money in a can back of the hog pen. Nobody gots any money in the bank except me and you, I'm guessin', and I ain't got much. You, Jess? How bad you hurtin'?"

"Not so bad, Pearl. I'll get by same as you."

"You ain't sayin' how much."

"Pearl, don't you be worryin'."

"That's easy to say. Hard to do. But I can do it easier than most. I didn't have much to lose, Jess. I'm just feelin' sorry for those folks. They don't have no money to pay their mortgages. Those folks will be feelin' this. There's some sad people today. They's all gathered 'round the ashes just a starin' at them. Some are purdy mad and want to hang the man and stretch his neck right proper." Martha sat down in the chair across from Jess, wiping her hands dry on the apron she wore. "Where's Newel?" she asked.

"Red's up at the Clarke place helpin' Far build a barn. Soon as I get back I'm gonna take him over to the Cooley."

"Good."

189

Lillian came running into the kitchen with Virgil behind her. They stopped when they saw their Uncle Jess sopping up milk with his bread. Jess eyed the two. "Which one of you two has been helpin' their ma?"

"Neither one," Martha responded.

"Oh, momma?"

"Well, who didn't make their bed?"

"Red."

"He ain't here."

"But he didn't make his bed, Momma."

Jess laughed. "I can see Virg is gonna be a damn lawyer."

Martha smiled. "Or a politician."

"I got some rock candy here for you two. Where's Joe? I got some for him, too."

"He's playin' with Ring, Uncle Jess."

"I guess he don't like rock candy."

"He likes it plenty."

"Well, go get him," Jess said, dunking the fresh baked bread into the cool milk.

CONVERSATIONS - 4

A shadow of a man filled the door frame.

"Uncle Jess." Lillian had looked up, recognizing him. Beside her, Joe and Virgil turned in their chairs, looking at the man in the doorway. Their mother was at the kitchen counter getting a dish rag. She turned to see Jess stepping inside the door way. Pearl ran to him and gave him a hug. "Come in. Come in," she said, pulling him inside the kitchen.

"Where have you been? Got everyone worried sick. Virgil, get Uncle Jess a chair. I'll fix him a sandwich." She paused. "Jess, you look terrible. Have you eaten?"

Virgil slid a chair around the table to where Jess was standing. Jess made use of it, slouching over, leaning against the table surface.

"All right, you three. Outside. Find something to do."

"Ahh, Mom."

"Get. Uncle Jess, he's tired. Find something to do."

"Jess, What would you like? I can make you a sandwich. I have some leftover potato soup. Would you like that?"

He nodded, looking at Joe standing by the edge of the table staring at him.

"Uncle Jess?" Joe said. "Do you have any more rock candy?"

"Not today, Joe."

"Ahh."

"I know how you feel, boy."

His mother grabbed Joe by the shoulders and pushed him toward the screen door. "Outside, Joe. Go outside. Find something to do."

Pearl set a bowl of soup in front of Jess with a spoon and some saltine soda crackers. He took them in hand, crumpled them, dropping the broken pieces in the potato soup. Pearl sat in a chair across the table watching him.

"Where have you been?" she asked. "Everybody's been worried thinkin' 'bout ya."

"Montana. Up around Big Sandy. Know of it?"

She shook her head.

"It's to hell and gone. Way up north."

"Whatever were you doin' there? I ain't never heard of it."

"Me, neither. Here," Jess said taking an off-white envelope from his pocket and handing it to her.

"What's that?"

"It's an envelope."

"I can see that. You ain't never written me a letter. So why are you writing me? That's what I'm sayin'."

"It's $45.63 cents, Pearl. That's what it is. If it makes ya feel better, I ain't writing you."

Pearl picked up the envelope, felt the coins slip to one end as she tore the other end open. Inside were four tens, a five and sixty-three cents in coin.

192

"Jess, you sweet, sweet man." Pearl paused, staring at him. "Whatever did you do? Or should I be askin'? What have you done, Jess?"

Jess laughed, sipping at the potato soup. "Sure you want to know?" he asked.

"No, I'm not but tell me anyway."

"Nothin' really. Let me set you at ease right now. I did nothin' wrong. I ain't killed nobody. That being said, after I left you a couple of weeks ago I went to the Palace Bar in Lovell and asked around. I was curious about what happened to my money. Talked to the man that sold our runaway banker friend a train ticket. It was one way to Billings. So I took a ride to Billings myself. Took me a big day to get there. A hundred mile ain't nothing to that Appaloosa. Rested up. While I was there foolin' around I had occasion to talk to another man that sold this feller another ticket--this time goin' farther north to someplace up around Big Sandy. I asked around and found where he was livin' and paid him a visit. Wanted to make a withdrawal from his bank, you see."

"He ain't got no bank. It burnt down."

"He ain't got the building any longer. A little light on records, maybe. I figured he took the money with him."

Martha sat down in the kitchen chair. "You could have been shot. Whatever did he say? Was it night or day? Did he put up a fight? Lord Jess, you're plumb crazy. Start at the beginning."

"As a matter of fact it was in the evening. He lived outside that little town. He was fixin' to sit

193

down and eat a little supper. Thought I'd be neighborly and join him, break a little bread together."

"Break bread. Jess . . . Jeez, I can't believe this!"

"Didn't work out that way. Seein' me, he turned all sorts of grey, got himself all edgy like he'd just run a five-mile foot race, keeping himself in front all the way and, in spite of himself, lost. Started telling me how he didn't have no money and how the bank went broke and because of the fire there were no records. He said 'there was nothing he could do.' Said that about ten times like I didn't hear it the first time. He was talking pretty fast so I had to pay attention."

Jess took a sip of soup and crushed some more Saltines. He smiled, thinking, looked at his sister. "I did tell him that if he reached for that short gun of his, I'd have to put a couple a rounds through his chest, ventilate him some. Told him that it would be hard as hell to miss at five feet though I suppose it could be done if I was real careless. I told him not to count on me bein' careless. That settled him right down. Lookin' down the barrel of a Colt .45 might of settled him down some, too."

"Jess, you're supposed to let the law do something. That's what they're for."

"Askin' a thief for my money? Didn't know that was against the law."

"It probably ain't but stickin' a gun in his face! That probably is."

"It's not like I advertised me visitin' him in the *Kane Herald.* I came horseback. I was careful. I didn't buy no tickets. I didn't leave no trail. And I had him lookin' down the barrel of my Peacemaker, all the chambers full, him owin' me money. He suspected that his life might be real short if he cared to disappoint. I felt plenty righteous askin' like I did. He did have my money burnin' holes in his pockets. I could see that."

"You didn't kill him. Or did you kill him? Is he dead? You said you didn't kill him."

"Now, hold on, Sis. Slow down. First, I told him about your $45.63. Told him how you'd be needin' it to buy groceries and seed for plantin' come spring. I told him you might be needin' a coat come winter. He said he felt awful sorry and that he didn't have it. I explained to him that he'd need to find it or I'd need to kill him and that my patience for thieves was runnin' a little thin. Hearin' my suggestion he pulled out his wallet and counted your money out on the table. I said I'd need it in an envelope. That's how it got in that envelope. I didn't want to lose it in my saddle bags."

Pearl shook her head and smiled. "Thanks," she said. "What about you? Did you get paid? Did he pay you?"

Jess smiled."He did. At first he told me how he didn't have $625.00. He said that several times. I said I didn't really care whether he had $625.00 but I expected him to get it. I explained how the real question was whether or not his life was worth $625.00. If not, I was prepared to send him to Jesus

195

right then and not give it another thought, knowin' he'd be in such good company and all."

"I can't believe you said that." Pearl paused, thinking. "Jess, would you have done that? Killed him, I mean?"

"It was my intention."

"He did pay you?"

"He did. First he did a little rememberin' 'bout where he had my money. Once he recalled, he easily located the money that he didn't have and paid me. He was pretty much convinced that I was goin' to kill him. I was of a mind to oblige him. I surely was."

Pearl stood, shook her head, her hands on her hips, staring at her brother."Oh, I'm forgettin' myself. You still hungry? Can I fix you a sandwich? I gots butter and choke cherry jam to go with fresh bread. Baked it last night."

"That'd be nice, Sis, and some milk if you got it."

"What about those other people?"

"They ain't my problem, Sis, I'd appreciate it if you wouldn't tell nobody what I did. Ain't none of their business. The best we can do is take care of our own. I'd like to keep it that away. Keep it simple."

Pearl smiled."Okay," she said, "I won't say a word."

"Thanks, Sis. Appreciate it. "

"Here's your milk."

First State Bank before it inexplicably burned down
and the banker simultaneously disappeared into
Montana.

CONVERSATIONS - 5

After the old man, Joseph Henry Howe, had himself a little farm sale, he abandoned the homestead at Himes, Wyoming. Having collected his money he forded the Big Horn River at Himes and flagged the train down on his way to Pasadena, California. He got a new wife and eventually got himself killed. He was hit by a car at a service station and didn't survive. The family moved to the Clarke Place at the foot of the Big Horn Mountain. Now it's called Moncur Springs. Estella (Moncur) and her husband, Will, lived there.

The rest homesteaded on the Duggan flat between Trout and Deer Creek on the backside of Low Mountain. Rose and Lee Hoffman homesteaded on Trout Creek. Jess filed a homestead claim and settled in Hannon's Cooley. Lou took a job ramroding for the Moss Ranch. His wife, Lida, did the cooking for the Moss outfit.. The family gathered at Jess' place often. That house was there until recently. It was used as a hunting lodge until the Park service tore it down and burned it up. It offended them

On the occasion of this conversation, Jess, Lou, Martha Pearl, and Rose were present in Jess' log cabin. Odd how they never lived very far from one another.

"How you like ramroding for old man Moss, Lou?" Jess asked.

Pearl passed Lou the gravy and a bowl of mashed potatoes.

"Better than starvin'. Cookin' ain't bad. Gotta say that."

Lou loaded his plate.

Jess chuckled. "Helps to be married to the cook. With Lida makin' your vittles you'll fatten right up. Have to get a bigger saddle horse and a new hat. Cows lookin' good? Plenty of grass this spring."

"Cows are lookin' good. Being in charge has its advantages. Sometimes it ain't good no matter what."

"Where's Lida?"

"Over at the ranch. She didn't want to come just to ride back in the dark. Somethin' bad happened to one of the hands," Lou began. "You know that ol' cowkid Long Frankie? Frankie Messer? That's his name."

"Yeah. He's a good one. From up there in Red Lodge. Know'd his folks. Good people. His mother was from Basin City. What about him? Get himself snake bit? Did you know he was married? Gots himself a woman." Jess took the bowl of mashed potatoes and passed them to Rose.

Lou nodded, taking a drink of water. "Yes, well he wanted to go see his woman down there in Kane. Hadn't seen her for three or four weeks and he wanted to. So I let him. Couldn't see no harm him goin' to see his woman."

199

Rose look at Lou. She said, "His woman? I know'd her, too. She was at that dance where old D.E. Bassett was playin' the fiddle. They were both there. That boy can fiddle."

"When was that?"

"That'd be last fall. It was a big dance. A box social."

Lou continued. "Long Frankie done made it home all right. Found some waddie comin' outta his front door buttonin' his britches. So Frankie takes a look at thet and sees red. Don't take much to set him off. He's like that Johnny Booze. Gets it goin' fast, he does. I reckon anyone would see red seein' that sort of thing right in front of him."

Jess said, "Saw Johnny Booze over in the Cookstove Basin a couple a days ago. He's lookin' for more graze. That fellow went clear to Washington to see them government folks. Said he ain't got no luck. Like talkin' to a wall."

Silence.

"What happened to Frankie, Lou?" Rose asked.

Lou shook his head, thinking before he spoke. He said, "Frankie sticks the steel to that horse's belly and he starts to chasin' this waddie around that cabin of his. He's a yellin', talkin' real mean, sure enough fixin' to kill that fellow for entertainin' his wife." Lou paused, looking for the salt and pepper.

"How do you know all that?" Rose asked.

"That's what the cowhands are sayin'"

200

Pearl interjected, "So did he kill him? I'd of sure killed him. I'd of tried."

"He didn't kill him, Pearl. 'Bout the third time around that cabin his so-called wife opens the door and throws that waddie a shotgun. Poor ol' Frankie gets himself blown right out of the saddle for findin' his woman with that fellow. Killed him dead. That's the way of it."

"Whoa!" Jess exclaimed. "Killed him?"

"She killed her own husband?" Rose said. "What a tart! Something was wrong with her. I swear."

"Frankie sure is dead. I ain't been feeling' good about Long Frankie since I give him several days off. If I hadn't done that, the poor boy'd be alive. I surely got him killed."

Rose stared at her brother. "So, what'd they do to that waddie?" she asked. "He get himself hung?"

"That's what's odd. He didn't. The sheriff was of the opinion that it was self defense on the account he was comin' out of Frankie's house and Frankie tryin' to kill him for entertainin' his wife. He's one worthless so'n so. Don't know how he got himself elected."

Rose said, "I can't believe she killed her own husband. What a chippy."

Pearl shook her head. "Nothin' you could have done, Lou. You're wearin' too broad of shoulders. Let it go. Nothin' you could have done."

"I'm tryin' to let it go but it keeps showin' up."

Jess said, "Don't let it bother you. That's senseless."

"Hard to forget. Life sure throws some curves, don't it? There ain't a rhyme to it," Lou added, shaking his head. "It's hard to figure he just went home and ended up dead."

"Lou, what are you talkin' about? It sure ain't your fault." Jess leaned back in the kitchen chair. He said, "Pearl, how's that pie shapin' up? Lou is gonna try explainin' how he's all responsible for Long Frankie gettin' himself killed when he ain't got nothin' to do with it."

"No, I ain't gonna try explainin' it. But it's disturbin'. Something just as disturbin' happened to me a while back when me and Forest were in France. That'd be in '18 'cause we didn't get there right away. It was nothin' too. But there I was. We got a caisson, a wagon stuck in this mud hole. It was pullin' a cannon, the back loaded with ammunition. Sunk down on both axles. Had two pair pullin'. Some boys pushin'. Some were gettin' a rope to tie into it. The Sarg, he wants me to get up on the box, thinkin' I could work those horses better than the Kansas boy that was up there handlin' the ribbons.

"He told me--he says, 'Bill, get up there. See what you can do.' I was fixin' to do just that and this round hits us. Kills the man on the box dead away. Nothing left to him. Never had a chance. Kills those horses. Nice horses, too. Kills the man standin' beside the wagon. There I was alive. Course I hit the dirt, but those men were dead. I wasn't. I was standin' no farther from that Kansas boy than that

202

kitchen stove is from me right now. It easily could have been me on that box holdin' the reins. I could have been dead. But I was alive and he was dead. They were all dead. The Sarg was dead. Never could understand the rhyme or reason for it. Luck, I guess."

Rose listened, nodding her head. "Lou, it wasn't luck. Pearl and me, we were prayin'. That's what it was. Both you and Far got home. She was prayin' every day. Never missed."

Lou nodded. "I saw Far when I was over there. Did you know that? You'll never believe this but I found him sittin' alongside a road. Nobody was around. He'd been shot up pretty bad. Bleeding from his side and leg. He was in bad shape and mad. Mad as I've seen him."

Pearl stopped chewing. "You saw him? I didn't know that. I haven't heard this story."

"Yes, I saw him. Spoke to him. Said 'Far, good Lord, man. . You ought to get some help. Get to a medic.' That's what I told him. Told him to get to the rear and get some help. But he wouldn't hear it. He found himself a horse and went right back to the front line bound on killin' some Kraut for shootin' him. He was mad. That's the last time I saw him whilst we were over there. Next I heard he got himself to a medic and later I heard he was sent home. He was sure mad. Got home before I did."

"Good for him," Jess said. "Wonder if he got any. Later, I mean."

"You mean kill some folks for shootin' him?"

"Yeah. Some Krauts."

"Said he did. Said he got some. Said he evened the score."

"Knowin' Far, he got more than one."

"Yeah, probably. He was mad; I can tell you that."

The tall, rangy man looked up from his plate. He said, "Rose, I'd like some of that pie now if I could. And if we got any cream, I'd like that, too." He paused, shaking his head. "Sometimes it bothers me. Sometimes I wonder why that Kansas boy and the Sarg and not me. That's what I wonder."

Rose said, "I told you why. Pearl and me did a lot of prayin' while you two were gone."

"No explainin' it, really."

"I just did. Pearl and me did a lot of prayin'. That's why you're here. 'Cause we needed you. She done prayed you home."

"I suppose."

"Pie?"

"Sure, Lou. Comin' right up."

"I ain't heard that story before," Pearl said. "What about the rest of you? You all fixin' to want some pie?"

Lou and Jess Howe
205

CHAPTER 14

MIRACLES AND MAGIC

September brings to the kitchen the canning smells of peaches, apricots, apples, corn and plum jelly. It brings messy counters, pots of boiling water meant to scald empty Kerr and Mason jars, and seal pints of buffalo berry, current, and Chokecherry jellies and jams. Instead of a kitchen table being filled with dirty breakfast dishes, its surface is a parade of colorful jars, clean and shining, full of the finished product. All waited for someone to take them to the root cellar, or to be stored on pantry shelves or into storage boxes that find their way to shelves in attached garages or safely cached under beds and seldom visited corners.

On the porch in Madge's house were four baskets filled with ripe transparent apples, six baskets filled with ears of corn still in their shucks, waiting their turn to be shucked, the plump yellow kernels blanched, then removed from the cobs with a thrice sharpened Old Hickory paring knife with its worn and stained oak handle.

All week this helter-skelter, hurry-scurry life had been repeated daily, morning until night. Each grain, each fruit, each berry waited its turn, and there was no time to lose. It was "must do now"; do it while the fruit is ripe and ready; "do it" before the

206

first frost turns the cottonwood leaves yellow. It could be any September day. This day in Kane, Wyoming was the second day of elementary school; it was the day following Labor day, attendant with crisp new school clothes, unsharpened pencils, unopened/unused tablets and tasty, to be chewed incessantly until they were gone or lost, white erasers.

Andy May was mad about something. Shouldn't have been. He had a new Chevy pickup parked in front of his white frame house. Madge, his other half, was standing at the kitchen sink, her hands in hot water, wondering how he was going to pay for it, how they were going to pay for it! She didn't dare bring the topic up, not when he was agitated like he was this day in September. Where was he? She asked herself. He'd given Greg, their first grader, hell about something

Afterwards Greg refused to go to school, refused to get on the bus when Harvey Nebel pulled up and stopped at the bus stop on the county road and flung open the door. Thank God everyone else that was supposed to, got on the bus. Minutes before it was hurry, hurry, hurry, the bus is coming, then it was there, Madge didn't have time to solve Greg's problem so he didn't get on the bus. Greg's problem? What problem? His dad was the problem. Madge threw up her hands. How was she ever going to solve Andy? She didn't know.

Water was boiling in the large kettle, heating on a propane stove, waiting for more Mason jars to scald. She filled it with glass jars, hoping that they didn't break when suddenly introduced to scalding heat.

Afterwards, she finished filling the jars on the counter with peaches, filled them with water almost to the top, turned the lids tight, then placed them in the pressure cooker. She dumped the peach skins and peach pits in the slop pail along with the milk strippings. She could hear Scotty playing in the back bedroom. Wondered what he was doing; not having time to go see. Taking a breath she dried her hands on a dirty dish towel then, looking at it, tossed it down the counter out of the way. I gotta get another one, she thought and went into the living room to find the basket of clean clothes.

Greg was sitting on the couch thumbing through a worn Life magazine. He looked up. "Mom, I'm going to take Scotty for a push in his stroller."

"Ok," she replied, already tired, a woman with too many things demanding to be done with too little time. She glanced at Greg then started going through the stack of towels, looking for a white dish towel; she found one. It wasn't all that white but it would do. Greg had Scotty's stroller and was pushing it through the living room toward the bedrooms in the rear of the house. Outside the dog was barking. He was always barking. Today, she hated that dog. It was one more thing. She could hear Scotty and thought he was in one of the back bedrooms. She wondered what he was using to occupy his attention. What could he be doing? He was born in January; this was September; he was nine months old, way big for his diapers. Already he was crawling across the floors, hoisting himself up on kitchen chairs, the edge of the couch, Andy's easy chair, and the TV stand. He was everywhere. It was good that Greg was going to take him for a push in his squeaky-wheeled stroller. Maybe by the time he got back Scotty would go down for a nap. If she were lucky, really lucky and the "damn" dog stopped barking, just for once.

Madge stared at the kitchen sink, the pile of yesterday's evening dishes, breakfast dishes, canning jars, cooking pots and pans, left over eggs and bacon, and the cat walking along the counter top. She shooed her away but the grey cat just looked at her and meowed, then sniffed at a cold strip of partially eaten bacon, ignoring the waving hand. Having smelled the dried bacon, she turned her nose up at it, then proceeded to smell the half full glass of milk. Madge knew what was going to happen next: the cat would tip it over, maybe break the glass, mess up the counter, leaving her more to do. Hurriedly, Madge picked up the cat, dropping it on to the gritty floor. It lit on all fours and scurried under the table, where it sat, licking its lips, looking up at her.

That taken care of she went to the porch and carried in four baskets of fresh picked corn cobs, lining them up in a row along the edge of the kitchen table. She emptied the first basket on to the table top, sat down and commenced peeling the shucks off. One after another, she placed the bare ears in a pan, dropping the shucks into the empty basket.

In the middle of working through the first basket she heard a noise in the living room; she set the almost shucked ear on the table and went to see what was going on. You never know with a crawling baby. Scotty could be anywhere into anything. She found Greg sitting on the sofa with a Life magazine, its cover torn, looking at the pictures.

"Greg, I thought you were going to push Scotty."

"He didn't want to be pushed."

"He didn't?"

He shook his head no.

"Where is he?"

"I don't know. He was in your bedroom."

Where was he? It's too quiet. Oh my. How long has it been? What, on earth, could he be into. I hate to think.

Madge hurried into the back bedroom, glanced about, then into the side bedrooms. Beds needed to be made; put it on the list. She listened. There was no Scotty. Next she glanced into the bathroom, looked behind the shower curtain into the tub. Where was that kid? Her concern mounted. Before she'd been interrupted shucking corn she was on the porch. She hurried outside to look on the porch. He wasn't there. She went back to the living room, opened the front door and looked out. There was no Scotty.

"Greg, have you seen Scotty?" she asked.

He shook his head "no," his head buried in the magazine.

"Greg, go look outside. See if you can find him."

"Ahh, mom."

"Hurry, Greg. Right now."

The six year old got up, set the magazine on the couch and started for the front door.

Madge retraced her steps through the bedrooms, kitchen, laundry room, finally ending up in the living room where she started.

Minutes later, Greg came back inside and said, "He's not outside, Mom."

"Where did you look?"

"You know, outside. Everywhere. I didn't see him. He's not out there."

Madge's heart was in her throat. It was far, far too quiet and it had been far, far too long. With a mounting urgency, Madge retraced her steps, this time ending up in the kitchen. There was no baby anywhere. Where was he?

She glanced at the counter, the doors to the cabinets. She listened. There was no sound of a baby. Greg came into the kitchen. She looked at him.

"Greg, go check under the beds. Look in the bathroom. Did you look under the truck outside?"

Greg nodded his head. "I told you, Mom, he ain't outside. I've looked under the beds."

"Well, go check under the beds again. Hurry."

Greg left the kitchen, heading to the back bed rooms.

Madge glanced out onto the porch then back into the kitchen. What was that dish towel doing in

211

the slop pail? She'd just got it out of the basket. And it had been clean. She must have dropped it; maybe it fell from the counter when she was stacking jars. But that doesn't matter. Can't worry about it, Not now. I've gotta find Scotty.

"Scotty," she cried aloud. "Scotty," she shouted.

She heard Greg calling his brother's name in the back bedrooms.

Shortly, he re-entered the kitchen, "He ain't there, Mom. He ain't in any of these rooms. He ain't in the bathroom."

Madge's worried steps took her to the sink. Where could the baby be? She glanced out the kitchen window then at the table where the bare corn cobs were stacked. She glanced down at the slop pail and the wadded towel draped haphazardly across the lip and down the side. Unconsciously, she reached down to pull it out of the slop pail. It didn't come easily. It was heavy, like it was soaked with milk strippings and whatever else was in there.

For the first time she looked at the towel. Really looked. Oh my God, she thought, gasping, not daring to think. She reached for the towel, pulling on it, jerking on it. Out came two bare legs, dripping milk strippings. Madge grasped the baby's soaked night gown and pulled him out of the slop pail where his head had been buried in peach pits, milk strippings, old soured Kool-Aid, partially eaten eggs and old, over-cooked bacon strips.

Frantically, she tried to wipe him off. His eyes were closed. He wasn't breathing. Off came his night gown. There were no signs of life whatsoever; his head dangled loosely; his arms offered no resistance, falling off to the sides like loose flaps.

Oh my God. Oh my God.

Madge worked frantically with the limp body. Nothing. Not even a whimper.

What to do? She ran outside with the baby in her arms. Andy was nowhere. He'd been gone all morning. She screamed his name and glanced about. Listened. Nothing. She glanced at the new pickup, pulled the door open, baby in one arm, and jumped into the cab, reaching for the key. Her foot jammed against the starter. The engine turned over and leaped into life. Before she shoved the transmission into gear, she stopped to turn the baby upside down, trying to get the slop pail liquid to drain from his lungs. For two minutes she worked with him, moving his arms, pushing on his chest. Some milk stripping leaked from his mouth but there were absolutely no signs of life. He look so very dead. His physical appearance sent Madge over the edge. "Oh my God, my God," she muttered. "What shall I do?"

Get help.

Laying the baby beside her, Madge grabbed the steering wheel with her right hand and shoved the pickup in gear with her left. Her right foot jammed the accelerator to the floor and she roared out of the yard, throwing gravel, leaving Greg standing perplexed in the doorway. Turning left on the county road, she flew past the Sotos, the Brusentos, the Burlington Northern railroad stockyards, racing the truck to the bridge that

213

crossed the canal. Help. She had to get help. She glanced at the lifeless body laying in the seat beside her, her heart caught in her throat. "My God, my God, she prayed. Oh please, please, please."

But there was nothing. Not even a tremor in the lungs, not a cough, not a finger moment. What shall I do. What?

She had in mind to stop at the Howes and get Dora but she saw Newel riding a Farmall H tractor coming up the county road below the house. He was near the wire gate that led into the field when she spied him, so she roared down the road, slammed on the brakes and skidded to a stop across from the old log cabin of little Joe Brocious. She jumped out of the cab, waving frantically, yelling at Newel to stop, not knowing whether he'd seen her, wanting to make sure.

She was hard to miss; impossible to miss: a crazy woman, standing in the middle of the road in front of her pickup waving her hands, beating the air into a frenzy, dust rising in a cloud behind the truck.. And he knew who it was: Madge, Andy's woman, who he euphemistically referred to as Magic. He didn't hear her screaming over the H tractor's steady drone but he could see she was plenty excited.

Slipping the H out of gear, he jumped down and ran to her.

"What's wrong? What's wrong?" he said.

She tried unsuccessfully to catch her breath.

"Madge? What the hell's wrong?"

"It's Scotty. He's...he's dead, he drowned."

"Dead? Where?"

She pointed to Andy's shiny new Chevy pickup sitting in the middle of the roadway, the engine running.

Red ran to the truck, glanced inside the cab at Scotty's lifeless body.

"Shit," he said, "Shit, shit, shit" talking to himself ,then glanced at Madge. "Get in. Now. Get in right now."

Red jerked the driver's door open and jumped in the cab, his nose assaulted by the smell of the new Chevy pickup truck. At the time he didn't notice. Waiting for Madge to get in, he seized the knob of the gear shift.

Madge opened the passenger door and was pulling herself inside.

Before she could seat herself, Red slammed the truck in second gear, tromped the accelerator then ran through the gears one right after another, spewing gravel and dust behind him.

He didn't stop when he reached the intersection of the county road and Highway 14A.

He revved the engine as he took the corner in second and glanced at the woman, the body of the lifeless baby in her arms. "Madge don't you stop working with that baby! Work with him. Hear me? Work with him."

They made the railroad tracks, whipping past the switch lights. Madge had the baby upside down over her knee pushing on his chest. Her efforts were in vain. There was no life, not even a whimper. Madge was beside herself. She glanced at Red. His eyes were on the road. They'd passed the cutoff to the Baxendales, the dirt road that led to Pete and John Gams, took the corner where the Bushes lived and raced up the highway past the Meyers on the left, and Tuffy Tippets on the right..

At the Tippets the baby made a sound, not a breathing sound because he wasn't breathing but a horrible deathlike groan from his lungs and mouth.

The Chevy passed the Harmons, made it to the top of the hill and the houses belonging to the Dillons, and Wambecks.

Red glanced at Madge. In desperation she looked at him at first without speaking; then she said, "What do I do, Newel? What should I do?"

"Madge, don't stop. Work with that baby! Work! Hear me. Don't you stop."

So Madge kept working with the small limp body; holding him upside down, dangling him by his feet, moving his arms, pushing on his chest, moving his arms again, repeating herself. She had him over her knee, pushing on his back, rubbing his rib cage. Over and over and over again.

Hopelessly, she glanced at Red again. In that iron voice he'd learned and honed as a Chief of the Engine room in the United States Navy, gruff and raw, without respect for tender feelings, oblivious of sensibilities, being what he was and had always been, he gave his orders. He said, in a voice slightly raised, insistent, "Madge, don't you stop working with that baby! Don't you even think of quitting. You work. Hear me? Keep working on him. Madge, don't you stop working with that baby!"

Andy's new Chevy pickup passed Bob Casttenes Welding and Metal shop on his left and roared into town, gearing down as he reached Main Street, racing quickly past Mayes Brothers Automotive shop.

He glanced at Madge; she was crying. "Madge. Madge, damn you. Get hold of yourself. Working with that baby, hear me? Work with him. You haven't got time for this nonsense. Work! Hear me? Work."

Madge nodded and kept working with Scotty's body, kept moving the arms, pushing on the chest again, and again, and again.

Red turned left on Montana Avenue at the Ford Garage, geared down, and roared up the street to Tom Croft's office, third building on the right. Fortunately, their luck held and the good doctor was there and not fishing. Madge was beside herself, way past frantic, way past desperate, working with nothing put a small prayer offered over and over and over. The baby hadn't breathed from the time it took to travel from Kane to Lovell: at least fifteen minutes and he suddenly he started. Somehow his lungs filled with air. No one knew how or physiologically why. For well over fifteen minutes, from before she'd yanked his limp body from the slop bucket, there had been no sign of life: no whimper, no groan, no cry for mother, for milk, for a rattle, for a baby toy, for anything. Yet rushing through the doorway to Tom Croft's office Scotty started to breathe, his lungs involuntarily filling with air.

217

Tom Croft didn't do what he always was expected to do, what eventually and finally forced him to move away from Lovell, Wyoming to Provo, Utah. He didn't work one of his miracles on Scotty. For an hour after the baby started breathing, he worked with the baby but the baby remained comatose. Except for that involuntary physical act of taking in air, he was simply a wobbling mess of flesh. After he'd tried to get Scotty to regain consciousness and couldn't, he sent him to North Big Horn Hospital.

It was ten-fifteen at night when the baby opened his eyes. He was hungry. He started crying. If he could have talked, he'd have noted how sore his chest was from the massage he'd received from his mother and the good Doctor Croft, literally for hours. He did know he was hungry and readily manifested that.

In the late evening, sometime after eleven, Andy made it to town and the hospital. He looked at Scotty, saw his blinking eyes, his legs and arms moving, a firm grasp on a warm bottle furnished by the nurses, sucking hungrily. He looked incredulously at his wife. "Madge, there's nothing wrong with that damn kid. There's nothing wrong at all. What the hell's wrong with you?"

Answer the question? Madge couldn't.

She was too emotionally spent; for the first time in her life, perhaps the only time, she had nothing to say. It wouldn't have mattered. Even then, afterwards, after all had been said and repeated, the only words she heard were those still ringing in her

218

ears. With those words she could feel Red's burning eyes, his incessant instructions, his orders: "Madge, don't you stop working with that baby! Hear me. Don't you dare quit. Don't you stop working with that baby! Hear me?"

It was close to midnight and Andy drove Madge and the baby home, a shovelful of stars overhead lighting the dark Wyoming sky. He was driving his no longer new Chevy pickup truck. All the way home Madge was quiet, listening to the hum of the engine, the wind whistling past the passenger side mirror.

In the driveway the dog was barking tentatively at the grey cat sitting primly on the back doorsteps as if it had no care. In the corral the milk cow was bawling for her calf, waiting to be fed. Yes, she thought. I can hear you, Newel. She held the baby close to herself, opened the passenger side door and walked through the entry of the frame house and into the living room. Behind her, Andy was flipping the ashes from his Marlboro cigarette, looking toward the corrals, listening to the milk cow bawl wanting to be milked..

Andy casually blew smoke into the night air, swatted a mosquito and took a deep breath. It was just Kane, another September evening, a Wednesday, a small miracle, an answer to a heart felt prayer. Maybe it was just magic.

Footnote: The preceding short story is a eulogy of sorts. My sister, Grace Ann Robertson, extracted a promise from me to publish this as a tribute to Madge May, a second mother to my sister. Thus, I have fulfilled my promise to Grace Ann. She passed away on October 28, 2017. It should be noted that Scott May, nine months old when this event occurred in his life, went on to a life of accomplishment: He attended BYU-Rexburg: played football at the college level: was a rodeo cowboy of some accomplishment; all this because of a loving mother who did not quit when faced with the task of preserving his life.

CHAPTER 15

REQUIEM FOR A HEAVYWEIGHT

On Wednesday, February 21, 2018, I went to the graveside memoriam for Rex Hall Nebel. Never thought I'd do that. Never thought he'd die. But there he was in a rather small box, sitting over a deep hole in the frozen ground in the Lovell Cemetery. It was cold. By one in the afternoon the thermometer was hovering around three degrees Fahrenheit. There could easily have been twelve or fourteen inches of snow on the ground with a slight breeze blowing south off the Pryor. The sun was up and it was uncommonly bright. There were no clouds and, as graveside services go, there were a lot of people. Most were dressed in black, either because that is all they had for such occasions or because black was death appropriate. I tend to think that is all these mourners had.

I stood on the outside of this circle of humanity watching. On the far east side of the gathering stood his three boys, their wives, and Rex's grandkids. On the north east corner was Rex's sister, Cameron, and a small group of people that surrounded her. I hadn't seen her in fifty years-- since 1964 anyway. I wouldn't have recognized her if she were standing right in front of me and said, "Hi, my name is Cammy."

The rest of us completed the circle. Folks were standing five or six deep. And my toes were beginning to have a tingle in them, getting cold standing in the snow. I noted that Larry (Ellis) and Bill (Baxendale) were there along with me; that meant three of us who grew up with Rex or tried to grow up together in Kane, Wyoming.

The preacher began talking. I glanced around. I noted that Rex's casket was a little over five feet long. I had the thought that he must be uncomfortable in that box; it being so small, so short. It dawned on me rather sharply that Rex was actually a small, short man. I thought *I'll be damned.* It wasn't the way I saw him; it wasn't the way I remembered him. Looking at that wood stained box, I realized that is the way he was. It was an epiphany of sorts. Something I'd never considered. What I remembered of Rex was an illusion of six foot eight, two hundred eighty-four pounds of pure muscle, bone and anger, a monster hiding in the shadows.

The Reverend Kurt McNabb was giving a talk about Christ and how we all knelt at his feet hoping for redemption. It brought to mind one element of Rex's life that I truly admired. Growing up, Rex only had to go to church on Easter and Christmas. My folks were of the Mormon faith so I went to church every Sunday, and midweek of every week, too. During the summer when Larry went to the Baptist Bible School, so did I. Before mother was a Mormon she was a Southern Baptist. Nothing like covering the bases. Don't know what faith Rex was but he didn't have to go to church but twice a year. He was so lucky and I was so envious.

The Reverend McNabb, a short man himself, turned the microphone over to the attendees saying, "Who knows Rex? I haven't seen him in a long time myself." One fellow mentioned that he knew Rex when he was five, went to Rex's birthday party. Rex was ostensibly five himself. This fellow rode the school bus to get to the party which was at Rex's home in Kane. In the evenings his house fell in the shadows of Katy's Nipple. He noted that Rex was the kindest "kid" he ever knew and how exciting it was to ride the bus. Rex's dad was the bus driver and anyone going to the party had a free ride. Funny how things work that way. Dorothy Nebel threw some parties for her kids, I can tell you that.

When Rex died, he was living in the same "party house," the house where he was born, except he wasn't born there. He was born in Lovell North Big Horn Hospital, courtesy of Croft or Horsely. In 1965 when the government bought everyone living on the river out, Harvey moved that house to Lovell and Rex moved in, living there until he died from a heart stoppage a week ago. How many folks live their lives in mostly the same house where they were born? Oddity that.

I remember the young Rex as being slightly overweight, quick to beat the hell out of who ever crossed him or who he thought crossed him, or who he simply didn't like. He had a crew-cut, a flat top. He was a James Dean guy that'd roll his cigarettes up in the short sleeves of his white tee shirt. There were exceptions. In our little group, Rex didn't ever push Bill: life apparently being too short for that kind of danger. During elementary school Bill and Pete (Gams) got into it every day at noon hour, at the double doors where kids were lining up to go inside for grammar school. They'd do each other bloody, rip each other's shirts, smash each other's lips and noses, black each other's eyes. Honestly, I loved watching them. They were good. In the end, Mrs. Baird would have them both by the ear leading them inside to her office and the consequences of the paddle. Rex saw that and Rex didn't want any part of Bill. I don't blame him. Rex stayed away from Bill. Bill had no fear. Mrs. Baird and Bill were buddies and Bill wasn't the least bit afraid of her. So "Bill having no fear" sums up Bill but not Rex.

It isn't like Rex didn't speak to Bill. During one of those summer years when we were collectively, nine, ten, or eleven years of age, a bunch of us were horse back, no saddles, bent on relieving the proverbial and actual farmer Brown of his fresh, hanging in the tree, ripe peaches. Rex was with us. Not a normal occurrence. Mostly Rex wasn't allowed around Bill. His mother so decreed. We got caught red handed and Mr. Brown had a shot gun. He self loaded his shells with rock salt. There was all sorts of reasons for everyone not to stick around, not the least of which was Mr. Brown being able to prove up his accuracy with his shotgun. And we were trying to escape but Rex couldn't get on his horse. He tried but the excitement was a little much and he just couldn't. Bill jumped off and helped Rex get on, but Rex slid off the other side. Bill, seeing the mischief, slipped off his painted horse again and again helped Rex back on his horse. We got away, alive and breathing. Thank God. Presently, all except Sexy Rex are living proof. Mr. Brown did get a couple of shots off and I'm not sure that Bill didn't get hit in the process of helping Rex. It was the first time that I thought that Rex might not be six foot eight and weigh two hundred eighty-four pounds of pure gristle, hard to kill, run a muck, muscle, the terror hiding in the shadows. It was bothersome for in the middle of the fray he couldn't get on his own horse even when he had to. It was a moment of clarity.

Growing up it is odd the way Rex affected me. He was tough, full of bluster, armed with anger and resolution. Always right behind him was his dad. Harvey threw me off the bus more times that I want to count. Only Bill walked home more often than I. He was a regular, traipsing along 14A. Certainly, I was afraid of Rex, afraid somehow I was going to offend him, get crosswise of him, get the hell beat out of me. As a result, when I left home I studied martial arts every day, for hours on end, moving though the various belts. I learned all of the black belt series, learned how to hurt, maim and destroy people until I realized I didn't like what I was becoming and simply quit, walked away. It takes too much anger to want to hurt people. This, too, was a moment of clarity.

One thought impressed me about Rex and that was his need, his willingness to do battle regardless of the size and ability of the opponent. In the nineties, I was visiting my folks in Lovell. I was at the Hyart. It was the first of July and there was Rex. He approached me regarding suing the Federal Government. He he wanted me to serve legal notice and evict the Federal Government from the State of Wyoming. I thought about it for about thirty seconds. It's not like the United States doesn't have a presence in Wyoming. Indeed, Washington owns three-fourths of the real property in the State. I imagined serving them a notice to quit and considered the fact that the statistical possibility of me evicting the Federal Government was far less than zero. It was a fool's errand. Not for Rex it wasn't.

Rex was bouncing up and down, wanting to get started, wanting to beard the lion, kick the holy hell out of the United States, throw its proverbial carcass over the hood of his Jeep and drive up Main Street, Lovell, Wyoming, his windows down, blowing his horn. I was staring at him. Amused. At that moment what I realized yesterday was maybe false. He was every bit six foot eight, two eighty-four, armed to the teeth, unrelenting and crazy as hell. This, too, was a moment of clarity.

There are a number of different weight divisions in amateur and professional boxing. Rex? All hundred forty-five pounds of him? Rex was a heavyweight. That's certainly what his boys thought of their father. According to them every birthday, every Christmas they were presented with a firearm; something that went bang. Those living east of the

Kane tracks, beyond the stockyards--they may say he was a relentless bully, a pug with no nose. Those who purchased fireworks from him, including all five of my kids, loved him, loved his generosity. They were amused, then awestruck, when he told them about their grandfather holding his dad's hand, patting it, as he died in the North Big Horn Hospital. Nothing is as it seems to be and this, indeed, is the requiem for a heavy weight. God bless.

MY Ranch house, Garvin Basin

CHAPTER 16

JOHN BOOZE, AN EDITORIAL COMMENT ON HISTORY

Eccentricity often gets center stage among the storied individuals who graced the seventy-year existence of Kane, Wyoming. None of the eccentrics ever lived on the streets of this now nonexistent settlement, but in the surrounding community. Frank Sykes and Johnny Blue are headliners.

After all, who do you know that never removed his Model 1873 SAA Colt 45 from his hip, that buried his wife and new baby behind his log house telling no one? Or, in Johnny Blue's case, was, according to my father and Harvey Nebel, railroaded by the Bischoffs into a declaration of insanity, shipped to Lander Mental Hospital against his will without ever being a harm to anyone including himself and, upon coming to grips with the intolerable situation, hung himself?

His mule managed to get a few blades of grass from the small two acre canyon in which John Blue lived, barely surviving. Of course those several blades of grass were not eaten by Bischoff cattle. If you have any knowledge of the south facing escarpments of Low Mountain where John Blue lived, you'd know that it's so dry grass doesn't bother growing and the two thousand plus head of

Bischoff cattle that ran on the Big Horn Mountain never missed a single blade due to that scavenging mule. In the words of the old, now deceased Kane community old timers, "It was a damn shame what those bastards done to him."

Just bits of history.

John Booze was another. He came to the Kane area in 1890. He was a South Carolina boy born in approximately 1875, a year before George Armstrong Custer took on the Sioux nation on Greasy Grass Creek in south central Montana. In 1890 Johnny Booze was fifteen or sixteen years old. By all accounts (and there aren't many) he was a "young'un."

According to Bill Scott in his short history, entitled *Pioneers of the Big Horn*, Johnny Booze started the MY outfit in what is now called Garvin Basin/Cookstove Basin. During the winter, that is a most inhospitable place. The Cookstove is north of Devil's Canyon. In winter, Booze couldn't get out over any of the four Devil's Canyon trails and was forced to cross the Big Horn River though Chain Canyon and Barry's Landing to get to Kane.

On one of those trips for supplies Johnnie Booze had ridden south past Bar Hill. Those steeped in Doc Barry lore would know Barry maintained a pole gate on the trail consisting of bars or long wooden poles, hence the name Bar Hill. This enabled him to control who got into the Dryhead country and who didn't. In the 1950s, remnants of those poles were still lying to the side of the road on Bar Hill.

Back to John Booze. One side of the roadway at that point in the trail was straight down, the other straight up. Johnnie Booze was astraddle a horse and trailed behind him six or seven mules, all tied one to another in single file. Some folks actually tied the lead rope to the tail of the animal in front so that the string of mules trailed easily. That practice had its dangers, especially if one of the mules tripped, or took to bucking, thus yanking on the rope tied to their tail. Such activity would open the proverbial ball and for a few minutes things would liven up. Other folks secured the lead ropes to the pack-saddle of the mule in front for the same purpose.

Johnnie Booze was going to Kane to re-supply and intended to use those mules to pack those supplies back to his ranch in the Big Horns. The last mule in the line slipped and went over the edge, promptly pulling the mule just in front of him, until he was going over too, and so on. Johnnie Booze lost the entire string of mules over the edge into the bottom of what became known as Booze Canyon.

Bar Hill and Booze Canyon are gone. Very few, if any even know where they are. Over the passage of time the Park Service or the boys in the fancy government trucks and green uniforms educated at Yale and Princeton and the University of Skullduggery, have made these places disappear. They've given them new names, a new face, or no names, and no face, disregarding entirely the history. In short, making a mockery of the people who lived, bled, sacrificed themselves, and died here.

231

Evidence? Low Mountain is now Little Mountain. Why? I don't know but old man Moss, when he got that splinter in his eye, rode off Low Mountain for medical attention. Not Little Mountain. Today he couldn't get home because Low Mountain no longer exists.

In the 1910s Lou Howe was coming off the Duggan Flat, crossing a creek on the east side with his family. His boy, Edward Vorris, was sitting on top of a pack mule. The mule jumped the creek, throwing Vorris into the air, kicking him in the head. Other than scaring him silly, it didn't hurt him. Those early pioneers called the creek "Kicking Mule." So did everyone else.

The ubiquitous governmental powers that came along in the 1970s changed the name to Bucking Mule Creek. Their response to any objection is: "It sounded better. It was better for tourism. It is none of your damn business; we changed it because we could. So sit down and shut up. Besides, the history of the people who lived here is only important, if I, the government, say it's important and it's not."

Admittedly these are just small items. Tiny little inconsequential bleeps of history played out on the world screen. The descriptive word is "inconsequential." Sometimes history is changed and forgotten because of need improvements. The Yellowtail project flooded the property and homes of 57 farming/ranching families, covering their lives and that of all those who went before them. Such destruction is unavoidable in the march of time, the need for greater flood control, and the need for generation of more electric power.

A fellow named Cal Taggart built the road up the side of the Big Horn Mountain on 14A, built it so steep that folks cannot safely drive down it. He thus put an effective granite roadblock to any sane person who might want to come to the Big Horn Lake to fish or bathe or eat a hot dog or spend their money at the grocery store in Lovell, Wyoming. In creating Taggart's "Killer" Folly, the more gentle road, built by our ancestors with teams of horses and slip-scrappers, was bypassed. Such places as Five Spring Falls, Jimmerfields, and the sawmill where the old buzzard kept the black bear on a leash behind the shed, drifted away and were lost. The old road didn't kill people every year, and it was slower to traverse.

History was bypassed by an idiot who claimed that more and more money would flow into the Town of Lovell if we just built a road with a "minimum" ten percent grade. In fact, less and less economic growth resulted. Ironically, a federal building is named after him, even though his fingers are still wrapped tightly around the economic throat of the Town of Lovell, strangling it.

History. Small tidbits. Something to learn from.

I suppose all of this is understandable, hindsight being what it is.

Ultimately though, who we were, even in the face of so called "progress," should be rigorously preserved so that each of us, and each succeeding generation, will know who we are. It would be easy

233

to say that these small concerns are of no import. Perhaps in the present "strive to survive" mentality they even seem a minimal aggravation.

Over one hundred years ago on September 16, 1830 an attorney named Oliver Wendell Holmes read a small note in the Boston Globe which informed the public that the Department of Navy was going to take the USS Constitution out into the Atlantic and scuttle her. For good reasons: she had been built in 1812 for the French War: her hull was rotting away: her guns were obsolete and rusting, making them dangerous and unusable. Her masts needed to be replaced. Her sails were rotting, tattered and torn. She was no longer needed in the coming era of bigger and faster battleships with metal hulls, and huge guns, driven by more sails, larger turbines and steam.

After reading the announcement, Mr. Holmes penned a three-stanza poem entitled "Old Ironsides." It was first published in a Boston Daily Advertiser and, subsequently, hundreds of newspapers on the eastern seaboard. The poem essentially dedicated the old girl to the "God of Storms, the lightning and the gale." The public outcry in the USS Constitution's behalf was ground shaking and formidable.

Today the old ship, whose nickname was acquired from British cannon balls bouncing off her sides, is the only active wooden sailing ship of the line in the United States Navy. She is manned by Midshipmen from Annapolis Naval Academy. You can go to Boston Harbor and see her, and walk on "her deck, once red with heroes' blood, Where knelt the vanquished foe."

History was preserved for future generations so they will know exactly who they are and exactly what price was paid to get here. So they won't forget. It is interesting to note that her six sister ships are gone, eaten up by the passage of time.

Our history, the history of the people whose mules fell into a canyon, who were kicked in the head falling off a mule jumping a creek, who were so damn tough they never removed their six shooter from their hip, who hung themselves rather than submit to the futility of a mental hospital, should also be preserved and protected from those with no regard for who we once were. Change is good, but history, itself, should never change. If anything, it needs to be protected and guarded from encroachment by the idiots who walk among us, who would have us forget our heritage in the flashy name of progress and the almighty dollar bill.

Big Horn Mountain Crew, Highway 14A

Forest Howe working on Highway 14A

Grading the Big Horn Mountain Road, Highway
14A under the watchful eye of Ring, the dog

Enjoy an excerpt from another of
G. R. Howe's western novels

TEQUILA
PROMISES

PROLOGUE

Low Mountain is a barometer of sorts, a theoretical thermometer that measures the ambient temperature of heaven and hell.

In winter the storms roll in from the west and the clouds hang low on her rocky, barren slopes. It is then that the scrub juniper and cottonwood disappear and vanish in the cold haze. Sometimes the clouds hang so low you can't see the mountain at all. Sometimes Winter takes a notion to explain how a man better bring a good heavy coat because it isn't listening to any whining.

"No," the mountain sas. "No more, not now." That's when it gets serious and the thermometer bellies out at forty below. That's when it's god-awful cold and Low Mountain disappears altogether. Yes, sometimes she's a barometer, a harbinger of how hell is going to feel to those not given to fire, who think ice will, indeed, suffice.

In the early spring as the days grow longer and look forward to summer and fall, Low Mountain isn't that way at all. On her flat, often rolling, top, the mountain grass turns green, sprouting up through the purple sage; the mountain sheep, elk and white tail grow sleek and fat. The rock dog plumps up, barking at most anything, not because he's alarmed but because he has nothing else to do. In the cool of the canyon, whose sheer walls raise straight up a thousand feet, the fish swim through the ice water of

Porcupine Creek, Deer Creek, and Trout Creek. If God ever took a vacation, he'd take it there. No one would visit him; He'd have it to himself. "Alone" is something. Some say "alone" isn't what it's cracked up to be; but those folks haven't ever been alone; they haven't ever stood on ground where only God has walked, where the fish jump on the line, begging to be caught; where the bugle of the bull-elk wakes you up to eggs fried over easy in bacon grease, with hashed browns, and apple juice mixed with a shot of tequila. Even God loves "alone" on Low Mountain before the winter winds blow cold and angry and the grey clouds fill the canyons and draws with the snows of January.

CHAPTER 1

August 1885.

It started in the early 1880s. They did not recall the exact year with any clarity. It simply didn't matter in the stories told or the number of fish caught. Henry Williams and Frank Rodriguez had visited Trout Creek in August for three, maybe four, years running. In August of 1885 they were camped on the south side of Trout Creek when they met the Indian. It was a dicey area, if border, breed, and birth has some meaning. The small, meandering creek was, at best, ten feet across at its widest. One side was Crow Reservation and the other, not so much. It was simply difficult to know where the reservation ended and everything else began.

Getting to the creek was strictly a horse and saddle affair. Staying long meant having multiple mules and pack saddles to carry amenities: a cast iron skillet, corn meal, salt, pepper, a box of matches and bottles of well packed, closely monitored tequila. A second mule carried cans of sliced peaches, smoked sardines bathed in mustard sauce, tin cups, chipped but usable porcelain plates, a canvas tent for inclement weather, Mary Carlos' tamales, a butcher knife, and fishing gear. These were small inconsequential items, but they assisted in the enjoyment of life camping on the back side of Low Mountain.

It was late morning when Frank Rodriguez, fishing pole in hand, found himself looking at the big Indian. The fellow was dressed in loose denim pants, and a blue plaid shirt that only threatened to cover an expansive belly. He wore no hat, a knife scar ran across his left cheek from the point of his chin to his ear; his jet black hair was long, hanging down in his face, interfering with his vision, yet covering his forehead and cheek bone on the right side; some strands reached his rounded shoulders. He wore huge leather boots whose tops reached hawfway up his calves. Those boots had seen better days. His belly partly hid the wide belt that kept his pants up. The Indian was an anomaly; not only was he big in stature, but he was quick on his feet and athletic.

Seeing the Indian standing in front of him barring his path to the stream was odd. Frank had never seen another man on Trout Creek other than Henry.

The Indian said, "Get the hell outta here. This ain't your creek. You ain't got no business fishin' here."

That simple statement drew the line in the sand daring Frank to cross it.

Frank glanced at the bucket of brook trout he'd caught that morning, then back at the Indian whose hands were cocked belligerently on his hips. This massive man stood tall, his chin sticking out. He fully aware that he was formidable, an immovable object that had to be dealt with.

"You can go to hell," Frank said slowly, staring at the Indian. "This is my fishing hole. I fish here. You don't. And I personally don't care whether this is Reservation or not." Frank deliberately stopped talking, pausing. "Then he said, "You the best they got?"

The Indian bolted toward Frank and took a swing with a huge right fist. He missed, but not by much for Frank was quick. He dodged, dropped his fishing rod, and took a swing at the Indian. He, too, missed. They grappled, stumbled, fell and rolled down the embankment very nearly falling into the icy water of Trout Creek. After that, it was swing, miss, swing, connect, roll on the ground, wipe the blood from the mouth and nose, and swing again.

Sometime after these exchanges had developed an intense, living character of their own, Henry Williams pulled his SAA model 1873 Colt revolver from behind his belt buckle, poked the worn barrel into the bright August sky, and discharged a round. The percussion echoed off the mountain sides and slopes of the grass covered hills, into the canyons and draws again and again.

Frank was smiling; it was as if he'd never had this much fun, never giving an inch, never backing down. Neither did the Indian. But the Indian was a little surprised. This man he'd picked to knock around didn't seem to be impressed by his size, belligerence, and bravado. What was amazing was that Frank never stopped coming no matter what he did. He hit him hard, yet Frank didn't stay hit. What was even more amazing was this fellow hit back. It took a few minutes, but soon the Indian realized he should have brought a lunch.

After these exchanges developed an intense living character of their own, Henry Williams, who'd been watching with some interest, pulled his SAA model 1873 Colt revolver from behind his belt buckle, poked the worn barrel into the brightAugust sky, and discharged a round. The percussion echoed off the mountain side, slamming against the slopes of the grass-covered hills, then drifted into the network of canyons and draws again and again.

The combatants stopped their engagement to lstare at him, trying to figure out whether Henry was angry, crazy, or just liked to fire his pistol and listen to the resulting echo. For a few seconds Henry's intentions were a mystery; the Indian readied himself to sprint for cover; Frank considered falling down from exhaustion--the inevitable result of absorbing the bigger man's swinging blows.

Their alarm was misplaced. Henry stuck the pistol back behind his belt buckle and wordlessly picked up a tequila bottle, and two empty tin cups. He handed one cup to each, poured their respective tins full, and stepped back. With a certain aplomb acquired from fistfighting in the morning, they drained their cups, getting little on their fingers. Henry promptly retrieved the tin cups, then stepped back. He looked at both and then motioned for them to get after it. From his safe perch he wordlessly watched the morning's entertainment.

Four minutes later Frank had again rolled off an embankment onto the very edge of the creek and was standing, one foot in the water, the other not. The Indian jumped down to where Frank stood and took a swing. Frank stepped back a few inches, causing the Indian to miss, and counter punched his ribs. The Indian turned slightly and went down only to pop right back up again, a look of anger and determination etched in his face. His knife scar and lips had turned purple and red from smeared blood and his pounding heart.

Simultaneously, both of the combatants were again confronted with the disconcerting percussion of Henry's SAA Colt. This time neither considered jumping, running, or falling down. Instead, they accepted the tin cups and held reasonably still while Henry filled them. Henry watched as they drained the contents.

Henry motioned for them to get after it, which they promptly did, each throwing the other into the cold water of Trout Creek at about the same time. They came up swinging, thrashing about. The Indian had Frank by the throat when Frank slugged him in the belly and tried to knee him in the groin. That failed. Instead he pushed him onto the Reservation side of Trout Creek.

"Now stay over there!" Frank ordered.

But the Indian didn't. On they went.

The pistol report popped against the mountain sides again, echoing down canyon and draw, calling a time out. Henry stepped across the water, using the exposed rocks of Trout Creek as stepping stones, handed out the tin cups, then poured them full. He watched the combatants drain their cups, etrieved them, and retreated to the south side of the creek. Another six minutes of a slugfest proceeded before Henry pulled out his pistol and called for yet another intermission.

Half an hour passed. The bottle was drained and another opened; neither man could stand without falling down. Undoubtedly, their unsteadiness of foot was due, in part, to consumed liquor. It was also directly related to sheer physical exhaustion, exacerbated by the thin air on top of Low Mountain. Six thousand feet isn't high, but it isn't low either.

"What's your name?" Henry asked the Indian as he teetered, looking up, his arms braced on his knees.

The Indian stared at Frank, his breath coming in short gasps. He wiped his nose and shook his head in an effort to clear it.

"Fleury," he answered. "It's Fleury."

Henry said, "You put up one a helluva fight, Fleury."

Fleury looked at him, hesitating, unsure of how to respond.. "Thanks," he finally said.

"Hey, what about me?" Frank said.

"Franko, in order for Fleury here to put up a helluva fight, you musta given him a helluva fight. He can't put up a helluva fight alone."

"Oh."

"In order for Fleury to fight proper he needs someone proper to fight. That's the way this fightin' business works. There's a balance. Either of you want some corn bread? Some canned, smoked, and dunked in mustard sauce sardines?"

Fleury looked at Henry and nodded. Henry handed him a plate, the porcelain cracked in spots.

He dished the sardines right out of the can he'd opened with his jackknife. Afterwards, Henry offered him a hunk of cornbread, which Fleury accepted.

Fleury sought a pine log and sat down.

"Well, who won?" Frank asked.

"Franko, nobody wins a fight."

"Oh," Frank responded again. "And I thought the last man standing won."

"Do you want some cornbread and sardines? Henry asked Frank.

"I want some fried fish rolled in cornmeal," he replied.

"Do you want some cornbread and sardines whilst I fry you fish rolled in cornmeal?"

Frank nodded, accepting the plate, the sardine can, and a hunk of cornbread. Frank sat down beside Fleury.

"That's one helluva swing you got there, Fleury," he said.

"I like your head butt. Ever use that in a real fight?"

"That was a real fight," Frank said.

"He did once. We were in Mexico," Henry said. "Not only knocked the guy down, knocked him plumb out. Franko has got a helluva head butt. Fellow was out, lyin' on the floor for half an hour. Franko does love to fight."

"Fight? He can't fight. That ain't nothing'."

"Nothing? Maybe so, but I'd say you can't see outta one eye, your bruised nuts ain't helpin' ya much, and your jaw ain't workin' right."

"Yeah?" the Indian said. "What about you? You a fighter or just a talker?"

Not me. I don't like fightin' but Franko, he likes it. That time I was tellin' you about—you see there were these three—Franko had one on each arm—and the third, he was leanin' into Franko, tellin' him all the bad things he was gonna do to him. Franko, he leans back and pops him in the noggin with his head. Knocks him to the floor. And he ain't movin'."

The Indian stared at Henry in disbelief. "What were you doing? Why weren't you helpin'? Three on one!"

I was helpin. I pulled my Navy, popped a round into the ceiling. Made for a fair fight—Franko takin' it one at a time. And that fellow on the floor—he didn't move for half an hour. Fight was over 'fore he wakes himself up."

Where you from, Fleury?"

"St. Xavier."

"I'll be damned. A religious Indian. I didn't know there was such a thing."

"Naw. Not so. I ain't Catholic. I'm Absaroke Crow. That's just where I'm from. You two come here and steal fish often?"

"Every year, second week in August."

"I'll have to be here next year. Make sure you don't steal too many."

"Hold your plate out. I'll give you some of those fish we stole. See how you like them."

"Maybe we can have a big fight."

"Maybe, if Franko is willing."

250

"Maybe we can drink some tequila after each round."

"Maybe, if Franko's tequila don't run out.

Fleury, held out his plate. Henry slid four fryers on it from the cast iron skillet that he'd used to bake cornbread.

"Tequila is a most necessary requirement, though," Henry said. "Wouldn't be proper fishin' without several cases of Mexican fire water."

That's how it was for these three miscreants on the second week in August when five days became ten, though no one counted; when stealing fish out of Trout Creek was better than pulling the same fish out of Deer Creek. Stolen fish tasted better. The two creeks were a mile apart, one sort of on the reservation and the other not. But it didn't matter. Frank Rodriguez never let such a simple thing interfere with a good fight, nor Henry with a good driThe nk, not in mid August when the fish were biting and the plump rock dog was barking his intruder warning to all who would listen.

That's the way it was. It's the way it had always been except when it wasn't that way.

August 1888

The second week in August 1888 Fleury didn't make it; he simply didn't show. Frank didn't say much about it, nor did.

Frank and Henry were regular cowhands, the sort seen anywhere from Fort Worth, Texas to Missoula, Montana. Frank Rodriguez was born about one hundred twenty miles north of Mexico City to Spanish parents originally from a small town outside of Seville, Spain. Frank had two older brothers: Jesus and Eduardo. He was three years older than Henry He could read and write and, when pushed, he could sing. He wasn't pushed all that often.

Henry Williams was born in 1844 in a one room log cabin outside of Danville, Illinois. He had a sister named Ellen, a dog named Ring, a mother named Rose and a drunk for a father called Fleece— no one knew why. Henry called Frank, Franko.

Frank was partial to leather cuffs, high crowned Stetson hats with a leather drawstring to keep from losing them in a wind storm, Bull Durham tobacco and a Copenhagen chew. He was light-skinned, burned brown by sun and wind. He spoke Spanish and English fluently. He could handle a riata like it was an extension of his right arm, wore boots to the knee--with the legs of his britches tucked inside--dog ears to pull them on, as did Henry. Frank called Henry, Henry or Hank. Henry didn't smoke or use chewing tobacco.

The crown of Henry's Stetson was not as tall as Frank's. He didn't wear leather cuffs. He didn't

252

like Spanish rowls. He didn't like shotgun chaps, did prefer batwings. He could understand Spanish, spoke it a little; did speak bad English. He stood five foot eleven inches tall, which was two inches taller than Frank. He weighed one ninety-five; Frank weighed two hundred and was a little more stocky. Henry didn't smoke or use chewing tobacco. He was known to drink a little tequila when the occasion called for it; Frank, a little more. Frank Rodriguez was defined by what he liked, Henry by what he didn't.

Both men came well heeled. Both carried Model 1873 Winchester rifles: Frank's bored for 30-40 caliber while Henry carried a 30-30. Frank carried two Colt SAA 1873 Peacemakers: one strapped to his thigh, the other tucked behind his belt buckle. Henry carried three--he being a little paranoid, having been raised on Navy Colts that were prone to misfiring and took forever to load. Sometimes he didn't have forever.

Pistols, rifles and ropes were as commonplace as ticks crawling on a horse's belly. Western men never went anywhere without shooting irons, but proficiency was another matter. Most didn't take the time; their waking moments were primarily engaged in work. Henry and Frank regularly burned up cartridges aplenty, having seen the disastrous results of not being able to shoot with accuracy. Both considered firearms to be useless and even dangerous if their owners didn't know how to used them proficiently. They did.

Five days into all-the-fish-you'd-ever-want-to-eat, Henry mentioned to Frank that he missed the Indian.

"Didn't he say he was from that Catholic town? St. Xavier, wasn't it?"

"It was."

"Ain't that north of here?"

"It is."

"What do you say we ride over there and see what's keepin' him?"

"All right."

Just before noon, the sun beating down from a blue sky, crickets and locust singing their aching songs, they saddled their horses, stored their provisions in the V of a tall cottonwood tree, and turned the mules loose to graze in a meadow south of Trout Creek. Then they rode for St. Xavier: riding across the Basin Pasture to where Chain Canyon crossed the Big Horn, following the Bad Pass Trail along the west side of the river and riding north toward Fort CF Smith. They arrived two days later at St. Xavier, Montana Territory.

St. Xavier wasn't much; it consisted of a general store, a livery stable and corrals, three log houses, and a fancy Catholic church with huge carved doors, stained glass windows, and numerous statues. Scattered about and among the cottonwoods were a dozen buffalo skin lodges. The exact number fluctuated weekly. One hundred-thirty horses ran out on the grass on each side of the river.

"Ma'am," Frank asked a middle aged Crow woman standing in the Paxton general store, "do you

254

know a big Indian name of Fleury? Do you know where we could f ind him?"

She looked from Frank to Henry, then, without saying a word, walked away.

The store clerk was a little more helpful. He said without being asked, "He's in the jail at Fort Smith."

"Jail?" Frank said.

"Yeah. It seems he knocked out the Sheriff's deputy. Hit him in the head with his head. Put him down on the floor for twenty minutes. I'm told it was something to see. Nobody likes that deputy."

"You saw him do that, or you didn't?"

"No, I didn't, but everyone else did. The Sheriff has him in jail over at Fort Smith. He's waiting on the judge to put him in Deer Lodge for assaulting a peace officer, being drunk, and disturbing the peace."

Henry looked at Frank, scratched his head, smiled--at what it was hard to tell. He said, "Well Franko, I guess we need to ride back to Fort Smith."

"What are we going to do when we get there?"

"Visit Fleury, I guess. He ain't gonna fish for a long time where he's goin'."

Fort CF Smith isn't that far from St. Xavier: eighteen miles as the crow flies, provided it flies straight and is not given to detours. It doesn't take long to ride that distance horseback: six hours on a walking horse, riding along the Big Horn River bottom They rode a quarter of a mile off the river using game trails, and avoiding the thick brush, the cottonwood timber, and the winding river as it bent back and forth on its way to join the Yellowstone. The fort was built in 1866 by the U.S. Army. It lasted two years, maybe a few days more. The other buildings that made up the settlement came later, after the Hayfield Fight, after Fort CF Smith was negotiated out of existence and the Sioux had burned it to the ground in 1868. The settlement was built along the river, for the most part off the flood plain, after the Crow Reservation was again re-established in 1869..

"Amigo, isn't that Fleury's horse?"

Frank pointed at a bay horse standing in the heat of the afternoon in an enclosed pasture a mile north of Fort CF Smith. It stood motionless except for the occasional switch of its tail as it brushed off deer flies, horse flies, and an occasional mosquito. It stood with six other horses, not all that good-- slightly overweight--examples of saddle horses determined by fate to live out their lives on the Reservation. Both Williams and Rodriguez stared at a big bay, noting a blaze on its face, a long white spot on its right foreleg, and a scar on its left flank where the horse had been branded while a colt.

"Gotta be," Henry finally said. "Ain't nothin' uglier Henry paused, staring at the horse. He said, "Do you think there is a separate breed called Indian- -one that is good for nothin' except eatin' hay and grass, and throwin' good riders? I wonder where

Fleury got that horse. Look at him. What's he good for? Can't get outta his own way."

It was Fleury's horse. The duly elected Sheriff of Big Horn County was keeping him with the city livestock while Fleury was holed up in jail awaiting trial and sentencing. Frank caught him with his thirty foot riata while Henry watched--not that Fleury's horse put up any fight. He just stood there while Frank built himself a loop and tossed it around the horse's head.

"What are you gonna do with the Indian's caballo?" Henry asked.

"I don't know, but it seems a shame to leave him here. He is not theirs."

"He ain't ours."

"Let's take him and ask the Indian. Best we can do is turn him loose somewheres so he can get some decent grass and get out of the cold when it turns winter. How long do you think they will keep him in Deer Lodge?"

"Don't know. I'm wonderin' if that Sheriff will even let us see him?"

"Guess we will have to ask. Can't hurt."

Henry Williams and Frank Rodriguez tied three horses to the hitching rail in front of the Fort CF Smith city jail. For a few moments they stood on the boardwalk in front of the Sheriff's office, looking the town over. A wagon with three kids sitting on the endgate passed by. A breeze was coming in from the south.

Fort CF Smith was a typical western town: Reservation town: blacksmith shop, livery stable, and a store that sold everything from needles to garden hoes, hammers and nails to a bolt of red cotton cloth.

The city jail was a two room log cabin; the jail housing the prisoners was in the back, the Sheriff's office in the front. Once every month the circuit judge came from the Crow Agency to dispense justice in the Sheriff's office. Until then, whatever prisoners the Sheriff collected during the intervening days stayed in the jail behind his office. Sometimes it got crowded--especially when the allotment money was distributed to the local inhabitants and they got into the corn liquor they weren't supposed to have. The jail section had no windows, while the Sheriff's office had two: one on either side of the door.

After he'd stretched, Frank adjusted the pistol in his holster, opened the door, and stepped inside. Henry followed, letting his eyes adjust from the bright sunlight by staring into the darkest corner. A big man wearing a red plaid shirt was sitting at a heavily scarred desk. A row of rifles and shotguns hung on the wall behind him--originally in a locked cabinet, but no more. Something or someone had broken the door and it had been removed. There were three kitchen chairs with high backs, and a coffee pot on a cold wood stove.

In the front corner there were three saddles stacked, as well as two ropes, and a collection of spurs dangling from nails pounded into the log wall.

A pair of batwing chaps made of thick bull hide was hanging from a wall peg next to them. A deputy was standing, leaning against the south wall, his face deeply bruised and colored a dark purple and green. It looked like he'd been in a recent fight and hadn't won. Henry wondered what the other fellow looked like; the deputy looked capable, ready to take on a griz and dish out some punishment of his own.

A familiar voice came from the rear of the building.

"Franko, is that you? What are you doing here? Henry, what's goin' on?"

At the sound of the Indian's voice, the deputy straightened up, no longer leaning against the wall. "No talkin' to nobody, Mex. Prisoners are off limits," he said. "Hear me?"

"No talking, amigo?" Frank said. "No talking to nobody? But I ain't said a word."

The deputy took a step forward. "You get the hell out of here, Mex, before I throw you in there with that damn Indian."

On most days it was hard to tell exactly might set Henry Williams in motion. He could be--well--a nice guy and then--sometimes, he wasn't so nice. In the middle of the exchange—maybe because he called Fleury a "damn Indian," maybe because he called Frank Rodriguez "Mex," maybe because they were both his friends, maybe because he had a short fuse having ridden for two days coming from Devil's Canyon, crossing the Horn at Chain Canyon, and following the Bad Pass Trail—he reacted. In that moment, when authority met with Henry's innate concept of what's right and wrong, the Sheriff and his deputy found themselves looking at the business end of two SAA 1873 Peacemaker Colt Revolvers. They were the sort that Bill Cody carried around to make himself look really good, tough, and mean in the *Wild West Shows* in Paris, France and New York, New York. That isn't to say Cody wasn't tough and mean, but those pistols certainly helped the appearance. It also helped that he'd shot Yellow Hand dead with a Winchester carbine for reasons he couldn't remember.

Frank glanced at the drawn pistols, then looked at his companion's expressionless face."Henry, what are you doin'?" Frank exclaimed, seeing the pistols. "Estas muy loco! My friend, it is not good manners pulling a pistol on a marshal. I think there is probably a rule against this."

"Maybe, Franko, but I figure that if we don't get Fleury outta this hole, we won't be feelin' good the rest of the year knowin' he's in here with these sonstabitches." Henry hadn't taken his eyes off the Sheriff.

"Now Sheriff," he said slowly in a grating western drawl, "real slow, you stand yourself up and drop that gun belt. I want to hear it hit the floor and I want to see you shove it under the desk.:

"Boy, you're makin' a serious mistake," the Sheriff said, staring at him, undoubtedly surprised by the pistols. He certainly hadn't crawled out of bed thinking some fool cowkid from Illinois was going to pull a gun on him today. But there it was and the barrels on those six shooters weren't wavering.:

"Not as serious as you're makin', not standin' up and sheddin' that shootin' iron."

The Sheriff obeyed relunctantly, standing up, up, moving slowly, aware that the situation in his office had suddenly turned from mundane to volatile. The men standing in front of him fully intended to break an Indian out of his jail.

An Indian?

The Sheriff was struck by the ludicrous nature of such an endeavor, shaking his head slowly. He tried, but could not remember such a thing ever happening before.

Henry said, "Franko, have that deputy shed his firearm and open up that iron door."

"What are we gonna do here, Henry?"

"Get the Indian outta there."

"Damn right," Fleury said through the bars. "Get me outta here. Please get me outta here."

"Then what?"

"Well, we sure as hell can't put these two in that cell. Not with all those Indians. Those boys ain't too happy. They'd kill 'em."

"So," Frank said, "let me see. How about we let all these hombres out and put the constables in their own little hacienda?"

"Right. Right. That's right. We let the folks in there out and put these two in their place."

"So we jail the jailers to save their worthless lives." Frank paused, shaking his head. "Aye yai yai, compadre. Have you thought this through?"

"No. Not at all. But we shouldn't get them killed savin' the Indian. But savin' their lives and

261

gettin; the Indian outta there—that'd be damn nice of us."

"Please, please," Fleury begged. "Please stop bein' so damn nice and get me outta here."

"Now, Fleury, do not hurry us," Frank said. "Es muy importante. We have to think our mistakes completely through before we make them."

"Hombre," Frank finally said to the deputy. "You heard the man, chico. Drop the irons, open the door, give me the keys. Let those boys out and get yourself in. Por favor, amigo.. Please."

"You're makin' a mistake, Mex," the deputy said.

"I know, amigo."

The deputy grudgingly dropped his gun belt to the floor, voluntarily kicking it toward Frank. He stared darkly at Frank before retrieving the key from the wall behind the Sheriff's desk. Grudgingly, he inserted the key in the iron gate and turned it. The mechanism clicked and disengaged. The heavy iron gate swung open, squeaking on its oil-starved hinges.

The deputy said, I'm tellin' you, you're fixin' to make a big mistake, Mex. You surely are."

"I know, amigo. I heard you the first time. That's why I thought it through so carefully."

About the Author

G. R. Howe was raised in Kane, Wyoming. He graduated from Brigham Young University with a degree in Political Science and went on to receive his law degree from John Marshall Law School in Chicago. He began practicing in Ventura, California in 1976 and pursued a career in law for the next thirty-four years, after which he and his wife, Joy returned to Wyoming to ranch, raise a few cows, and write western novels.